"Let's start [...]
with our firs [...]

"What's that?" Abby asked.

"Honesty. If I don't understand something you say, I'll ask you. You do the same with me."

"I like that rule."

"Good. Now, what should be our next rule?"

"We make this fun for the teens and for ourselves. If we act as if this is drudgery, the kids will sense it, and we'll lose our chance to help them."

"Fun?" David arched his brows as if responding to something he'd heard in his head, then sighed. "That may be harder for me to follow than the first rule. Nobody's ever described me as fun. In fact, the opposite."

"Well, then we'll have to see how we can change that, ain't so?"

He gave her the faintest grin, but she took it as a victory. As they continued to talk about possible activities for the youngsters, she couldn't doubt he cared about his daughter and her friends. He was a man of strong emotions, though he tried to hide that fact. She couldn't help wondering why.

Jo Ann Brown has always loved stories with happily-ever-after endings. A former military officer, she is thrilled to have the chance to write stories about people falling in love. She is also a photographer and travels with her husband of more than thirty years to places where she can snap pictures. They have three children and live in Florida. Drop her a note at joannbrownbooks.com.

Books by Jo Ann Brown

Love Inspired

Green Mountain Blessings

An Amish Christmas Promise
An Amish Easter Wish

Amish Spinster Club

The Amish Suitor
The Amish Christmas Cowboy
The Amish Bachelor's Baby
The Amish Widower's Twins

Amish Hearts

Amish Homecoming
An Amish Match
His Amish Sweetheart
An Amish Reunion
A Ready-Made Amish Family
An Amish Proposal
An Amish Arrangement

Visit the Author Profile page at Harlequin.com for more titles.

An Amish
Easter Wish

Jo Ann Brown

LOVE INSPIRED
INSPIRATIONAL ROMANCE

LOVE INSPIRED®
INSPIRATIONAL ROMANCE

Recycling programs
for this product may
not exist in your area.

ISBN-13: 978-1-335-55353-9

An Amish Easter Wish

Copyright © 2020 by Jo Ann Ferguson

All rights reserved. No part of this book may be used or reproduced in any manner whatsoever without written permission except in the case of brief quotations embodied in critical articles and reviews.

This is a work of fiction. Names, characters, places and incidents are either the product of the author's imagination or are used fictitiously. Any resemblance to actual persons, living or dead, businesses, companies, events or locales is entirely coincidental.

This edition published by arrangement with Harlequin Books S.A.

For questions and comments about the quality of this book, please contact us at CustomerService@Harlequin.com.

Love Inspired
22 Adelaide St. West, 40th Floor
Toronto, Ontario M5H 4E3, Canada
www.Harlequin.com

Printed in U.S.A.

Let your light so shine before men,
that they may see your good works,
and glorify your Father which is in heaven.
—*Matthew* 5:16

For Justin and Mikayla, who are writing a beautiful love story of their own.

Chapter One

Evergreen Corners, Vermont

"Is he here yet?" Abby Kauffman called.

The freezer couldn't have picked a worse time to stop working. Supper must be served in three hours, and nothing was started. Worse, tonight was supposed to be a festive gathering for the local teen volunteers and their families, as well as those from Amish Helping Hands who'd come to help rebuild the small town.

Abby scanned the list of food stored in the freezer and sighed. It might not be an accurate list because she and the other volunteers working in the community center's kitchen had made it from memory. Nobody wanted to lift the top of the chest freezer and peer inside to count the boxes of meat and frozen vegetables and tomato sauce. A specific inventory wasn't necessary.

With hundreds of dollars of donated food inside the freezer, every minute counted.

She went to the wide pass-through window from the kitchen to the main room of the community center. A trio of young people were lounging among the collection of mismatched tables and chairs where the volunteers had their meals. She'd lost count of the number of breakfasts, lunches and suppers they'd served since the October flood five months ago had washed away houses and businesses along Washboard Brook and damaged more buildings farther from its banks.

So tonight, in addition to the ten to fifteen volunteers who needed to be fed at each meal, there would be almost twice that number joining them for a roast beef dinner with the fixings. The meat had been thawed, but the volunteers' favorite part of the meal—the pies—were in the freezer. Digging through the containers inside to find the unbaked pies would mean allowing precious cold air to escape, threatening the rest of the food stored in the chest freezer.

Where was the repairman? She'd found his name on a list in the community center office and called. He'd said he'd be there as soon as he could, and that had been almost two hours ago.

She put her hands on the counter and looked toward the door. When she hit her head on the pass-through, she grimaced and rubbed her heart-shaped white *kapp*. She was only a few inches over five feet tall, so she wasn't used to having to duck. One of these days, she was going to remember how low the top of the window was and stop bumping her head on it.

How she wished she could be more like her older brother! Isaac never overlooked a single detail about anything. She'd heard one of the residents of their small Vermont town, far to the north of Evergreen Corners, describe her brother as having a laser focus. She couldn't agree more. When Isaac was involved, nobody had to worry about the smallest item being forgotten.

Isaac was at home on the family farm, and she was working in the community center kitchen in Evergreen Corners for at least the next six weeks. If needed, she would stay on, though that might not make her family happy. She couldn't walk away when people needed her here. Since her *daed* had recently remarried, she no longer had to take care of the household as she'd done since her *mamm*'s death almost twenty years ago. Her stepmother, Lovina, was a skilled cook and housekeeper who could handle everything on her own.

And, more important, in Evergreen Corners, Abby could avoid anyone who reminded her of the worst days of her life, days after her self-ishness almost caused a young man's death. Busying herself with work allowed her to pay forward to others the blessing she'd been given, a blessed reprieve when the young man recovered. She kept on working, day after day, because she couldn't forget her guilt about how her foolish decision had nearly led to tragedy.

"Is he here yet?" Abby called again as she came out into the main room.

As if on cue, the outside door opened. A man she didn't know stepped in. Seeing he carried a battered metal toolbox, she opened her mouth to tell him to hurry to the kitchen and check the freezer before the food began to defrost, but no sound emerged as she stared.

He moved with the ease of a man who was comfortable with his long limbs. His shoulders were muscular beneath his unzipped coat. Black hair was ruffled by the cap he'd removed as he'd entered, and a single curl dropped across his forehead toward his full eyebrows. His eyes, as brilliant blue as a spring sky, looked around the room.

"Are you the repairman?" Abby managed to ask before his gaze reached her. She scolded herself for reacting like a hormonal teenager at the sight of a *gut*-looking man.

And an *Englischer* at that!

Isaac would be more than annoyed if he heard she was gawking at an *Englischer* with her mouth open like a fish pulled from a pond.

The man glanced her way. He took note of her plain clothes and *kapp*, and his assertive brows lowered in a frown. However, his voice, as he spoke, was a pleasant baritone. "I'm David Riehl." He crossed the room and held out a business card with words and logo to match the ones embroidered on his coat. "Riehl's Appliance Repair."

Startled how her fingers trembled as she reached for the card, Abby nodded. Again, she didn't trust her voice. She stored the card in the pocket of the black apron covering her dark green dress and motioned toward the kitchen. She walked in that direction, aware with every molecule how David followed a few paces behind her.

As they entered the kitchen, voices burst out behind her. Had the teenagers waiting to hear where they were working today gone silent when David entered, or had she been so focused on the handsome man that her other senses had stopped working?

Abby gave her thoughts a *gut* shake. She should be thinking of one thing: getting the freezer fixed. She stepped aside as he put his toolbox on the floor and walked around the freezer that sat in ominous silence. When he asked about the brand and model number, she answered, glad he hadn't yanked up the top to look.

Her shoulders eased from their taut line. David Riehl of Riehl's Appliance Repair knew what he was doing. Sending up a quick prayer of thanks, she watched as he put his hand on the freezer. She guessed he was searching for any vibration to give him a clue why the freezer wasn't working.

"When did you notice a problem?" he asked, not looking at her.

"It was running this morning. Then the compressor stopped, and it didn't start again."

"That could be caused by a few things, but let's look at the obvious ones first." He pulled a small flashlight from beneath his coat and switched it on. "I'll check the evaporator coils first. Dust and dirt get on them. It's almost like you're suffocating the unit because moisture can't evaporate. That may keep the compressor from starting."

"Our kitchen is clean."

He arched his brows before squatting to peer behind the freezer. "Even the best housekeepers forget to keep the coils clean."

"Or sweep under the refrigerator."

"Exactly." He tilted his head and glanced at

her with a cool smile. "I don't mean to insult you or any of the volunteers. We appreciate you coming here to help." He shifted the flashlight to examine the freezer from another angle. "Looks pretty dust-free."

Straightening, he moved around to the other side and reached to pull the plug out of its outlet.

"Must you unplug it?" Abby asked.

"If I don't want to get zapped, yes." When he smiled this time, it wasn't as icy as the interior of the freezer should have been. She wouldn't describe his expression as warm, but at least it seemed genuine. "Don't worry. It won't take long to do a diagnostic on the freezer, and you said when you called the shop the contents are tightly packed. That should keep them cold far longer than you expect."

"I hope so."

When David didn't answer but bent to unscrew an access panel on the side of the freezer, Abby knew she was in the way. He didn't need her standing behind him, watching everything he did.

She went to the two stoves and turned the ovens to 325 degrees. The beef roasts cooked in aluminum foil at a low temperature, giving the juices time to mix with onion soup mix and mushrooms to flavor the roast. On the table, four pans she'd lined with foil waited. Putting meat in each pan, she began to slice the mushrooms she'd washed before she realized the freezer was silent. She'd taken packets of onion soup mix from the pantry and was opening them when David spoke.

"Looks like you've got a bad thermostat." He put an electronic tester in his toolbox. Standing, he added, "I brought one along because that's a pretty common problem with older chest freezers."

"Is it quick to fix?" She sprinkled the mix over the meat and mushrooms.

He nodded. "Your freezer should be working in about fifteen minutes. I'll be right back."

"Thank the *gut* Lord," she breathed with relief as he left. When was the last time she'd taken a complete breath? Since the freezer had stopped working? Since David had walked through the door?

She was startled by that thought. He was an *Englischer* and terse almost to the point of being rude. Because he was easy on the eyes didn't mean she should see him as anyone other than skilled hands to get the freezer working again. She was glad she wasn't watching the door when it opened and his strong, assertive footsteps crossed the tiled floor.

He didn't say anything as he went to the freezer and knelt beside it. His broad hands navigated the small space afforded by the access panel as he removed the useless thermostat.

Abby averted her gaze again. She shouldn't be studying each of his motions, though she was fascinated by his knowledge of how the wires should be handled. Now wasn't the time to ask her usual questions about the way things worked.

The front door opened again and a cacophony of footsteps burst into the community room.

She smiled, knowing more of the teenage volunteers had arrived. On any day, about a half dozen boys and girls offered their time to assist the adult volunteers. She knew they wished they could climb on rafters to raise roofs or use the excavation machinery. However, the policies of Amish Helping Hands and the Mennonite Disaster Service and other organizations limited the teens to working on the ground. They could climb a ladder to paint a ceiling, but nothing more dangerous.

"Hey, what's going on?" asked Jack Gundersen as he stretched through the pass-through window to peer into the kitchen. The teen, who'd been one of the first to ask to help with rebuilding houses swept away by the flood, hadn't lost his enthusiasm in spite of weeks of hard work. He and his best friend, Reece Maddox, put in several hours of work each day after school and on Saturdays.

Abby smiled at the boys. Anyone looking at them might dismiss them as trouble because of their tattoos and cropped hair, but she'd come to see they had generous hearts. She didn't understand why anyone would ink their arms with identical verses from Proverbs 17, as the boys had done. Yet she admired their faith and friendship that had led them to put the words *A friend loveth at all times, and a brother is born for adversity* on the insides of their forearms.

"Something went wrong with the freezer," she said in answer to Jack's question. "The thermostat. It's getting fixed by—"

"Hi, Mr. Riehl!" called Reece, leaning next to his friend on the counter. "Anything we can do to help?"

"Just finishing," David said without looking at them. "But thanks."

"Are you and Mikayla coming tonight?" Jack asked.

Abby looked from the boys to the man kneeling by the freezer. She knew only one girl by that name. Mikayla St. Pierre was the newest teen volunteer, a pretty, quiet girl who liked to work alone. Someone had told Abby the thirteen-year-old was an orphan after her sole surviving parent, her *daed*, had died in a car accident and she now lived with a guardian. Was David Riehl the one who'd taken her in? Maybe there was more to him than the curt man who looked at her as if she'd come from another planet.

David reached into the freezer, his face turned away. "Tonight? What's tonight?"

"The volunteer supper." Jack grinned. "Roast beef and the fixings."

"And desserts." Reece's smile was broader than his friend's. "Lots and lots of yummy desserts. Isn't that right, Abby?"

She heard an odd sound behind her. Turning, she discovered David regarding her with a strange expression. She wasn't sure if he was upset or surprised or something else.

"Is everything okay?" she asked.

Instead of answering her, he asked a question of his own, *"You* are Abby?"

"Ja." When he continued to stare with indecipherable emotion glowing in his eyes, she hurried to add, *"Es dutt mir leed."* She flushed anew, not wanting to admit his presence had unsettled her enough to forget to speak in English. "I mean, I'm sorry. I should have introduced myself when you arrived. I was in a hurry to get the freezer fixed. Is it all right now?"

Again, he acted as if he hadn't heard a word she'd spoken. *"You* are Abby? Abby Kauffman?"

Concerned by his odd behavior, she wasn't sure what might be wrong with him. Moments ago he'd acted curt but polite, as she'd expected a busy repairman to act. Now he was gawking at her as if she'd grown a second head. What had she said to cause him to react as he was?

She couldn't halt herself from asking, "Are *you* all right, David?"

No, I'm not.

David Riehl was glad the woman standing between him and the door into the main room couldn't read his mind. Or maybe it didn't matter because his thoughts were so jumbled he didn't know how to sort them out.

Abby Kauffman—the Abby Kauffman whom Mikayla had mentioned over and over—was Amish? He'd assumed... He wasn't sure what he'd assumed, but he'd never guessed the name belonged to an Amish woman.

There was no doubt she lived a plain life. Her shimmering blond hair was pulled into a tight coil beneath a heart-shaped organdy head covering.

A *kapp*, whispered a memory from the depths of his mind. He couldn't remember what the pinafore-type apron was called. The color of her dress reminded him of pine needles, and her eyes were the color of a tree-covered mountain on a foggy day. Not quite green and not quite gray.

He shouldn't be staring at her, but he couldn't pull his gaze away. There was something undefinable about her that drew his eyes. Something more than her pretty features or her plain dress. He couldn't figure out what it was and, for a man who spent his life getting to the bottom of problems, not being able to put his finger on what intrigued him was unsettling.

David mumbled under his breath, hoping she'd think he was impatient to install the new thermostat. His fingers were clumsy because knowing Mikayla's Abby was Amish bothered him more than he'd guessed. He tried to concentrate on his task. It was almost impossible because his thoughts flew in every possible direction.

As they had too often since the night ten months ago when he'd gotten the call that Boyd St. Pierre, his best friend since they'd gone to Evergreen Corners High School together and a single parent after his wife died in childbirth, was dead. A slick mountain road, a careless driver and a ten-car pileup left four people dead and twice that many injured. Mikayla hadn't been hurt other than bruises and blackened eyes from the airbag.

David had had the air knocked out of him almost as hard by the shock of discovering Boyd had named him Mikayla's guardian. What did a bachelor who was an only child know about raising a thirteen-year-old girl?

At first, the necessary flurry of a funeral and settling his friend's estate and handling insurance claims had kept him too busy to think, but in the past couple of months, the pace had slowed to something similar to normal. He'd come to realize, though, he had no idea how to be a parent to a teenager.

Mikayla didn't talk much, but on the few occasions she did, almost every comment contained Abby's name. When she'd joined the other young people from their community church in volunteering, he'd been glad to see her spending time with people her age. However, he couldn't remember more than a handful of times when she'd mentioned any of the teens by name.

Just Abby.

Always Abby.

"Are you okay?" Abby asked again, ripping him away from his uneasy reverie.

"Fine, fine." It wasn't a lie. He was doing as fine as he could in this odd situation.

Why, among everything else Mikayla had said about Abby being so welcoming and fun and funny, had she failed to mention Abby was Amish?

As he finished affixing the thermostat and reached for the access panel cover to screw it into place, he knew the answer to his question. Mikayla hadn't said anything because being Amish didn't mean anything to her other than it was part of Abby's identity.

It did to him. He could hear his father's voice, low and filled with anger, deriding the ultra-conservative Pennsylvania Amish community where their family had lived for generations. David's parents had left when he was about to start school, so his memories of what had happened were fuzzy and contradictory.

"We were chased away by closed minds and open mouths," his father had said so often the words were imprinted on David's brain. Neither of his parents had spoken about why they'd abandoned family and friends and moved to Vermont, but they'd never taken any pains to hide their disgust with the Amish.

"Hey, Mikayla!" Jack pushed away from the window. "Did you take a bath in Pepto-Bismol?"

Mikayla appeared in the doorway to the kitchen. The stylish glasses perched on the end of her nose were pocked with bright pink as were her worn T-shirt and jeans. She was a slender girl of medium height who looked like her mother. A mass of brown curls surrounded her face that was dotted with enough freckles to be cute.

"Hi, Abby," she said with the shy smile he'd seldom seen. It vanished as she noticed him by the freezer. "Oh, David."

He waited for her to say more. She didn't. Instead she wrapped her arms around herself and stayed in the doorway. The boys by the pass-through window seemed as much at a loss for what to do or say as he was.

Abby, however, walked over to Mikayla and put an arm around her shoulders. "I was so hoping you'd drop in today. Have you enjoyed painting Kaylee Holst's bedroom? Every five-year-old wants a candy-pink room, ain't so?"

"It's been fun, but I don't know if I ever want to see pink again." Mikayla didn't push her hair back from her face, hiding her expression.

From him or from everyone?

David watched as Abby steered the girl he called his daughter, for lack of a better word, across the kitchen to the table where she was preparing the roasts. She chattered with Mikayla as if they'd been friends for years.

His fingers curled, his nails cutting into his palms. He should have been aware that Mikayla had become friends with an Amish woman. He prided himself on knowing the facts, so he could plan ahead. That skill served him well as a repairman and in life…until Mikayla had become part of it. He'd made it clear he was available whenever she wanted to talk. He'd changed his life insurance and made a will to provide for the girl in case something happened to him. He'd started a college fund for her, though she didn't want to talk about going.

He'd never considered she'd choose an Amish woman to turn to. He had to find out more about Abby Kauffman. The last thing he needed now was to have the fragile girl being judged as cruelly by the Amish as his parents had been.

Chapter Two

David gathered the tools he'd used and stored them in the toolbox. He tossed the old thermostat in a nearby trash can. The freezer was humming, a sure sign the problem had been solved. Usually he felt a sense of satisfaction when he confronted a problem, evaluated the situation, considered the facts and found a solution.

Not this afternoon. He felt nothing but utter confusion, which was growing by the minute like dandelions would in a few months across his lawn.

He watched as Mikayla chopped garlic and sprinkled it on the roasts while Abby closed the foil over them. He hadn't guessed Mikayla knew how to do that.

He didn't know because he hadn't asked her. He'd gotten used to the silence in his house broken only by the television. Before Mikayla had moved in, he hadn't watched it much, but he'd assumed she, as a teen, would have a variety of shows she followed. If she did, she must be watching them another way, because she spent most evenings in her room with her headphones on.

His daughter wasn't wordy with Abby, but she was giving the Amish woman more than the yes or no answers he got.

"Are you okay?"

At Abby's question, David flinched. He hadn't noticed the roasts had been put into the ovens and the preparation table cleaned. Mikayla was in the other room and he hadn't seen her leave the kitchen. He wasn't cut out to be a parent if he couldn't keep an eye on one teenage girl when she was standing right in front of him.

"David?" Abby prompted him.

"I think I'm done here," he replied, knowing she couldn't guess how he meant those trite words. He berated himself. Self-pity wouldn't get him—or Mikayla—anywhere. Boyd must have expected David to give her a family, but after ten months, the girl was still pretty much a guest in his house.

"How much do we owe you?" Abby asked as she opened the fridge and pulled out two dozen eggs.

"Don't worry about it."

She set the cartons on the table. "But you provided the part as well as your time."

"I'm glad to be able to help you. You're doing so much for my neighbors."

When her eyes widened and then warmed with gratitude, an answering smile tugged at his lips. He halted it. Because he wanted to do his part in helping with the flood recovery efforts didn't mean he should toss aside a lifetime of listening to his parents' stories about how they'd been banished by their Amish kin and friends from the only world they'd known.

Abby smiled as she wiped her hands on her black apron and he knew she had no idea what he was thinking. That was for the best. She hadn't done anything out of line.

Yet.

"That's kind of you, David," she said before bending to get a deep bowl from a cupboard near the table. "*Danki* for sharing your knowledge and your time."

"You're welcome." He couldn't help being flustered by the brilliance of her smile and the way her face glowed with a sincerity he couldn't doubt. Someone had told him the various Amish volunteers in town had come from different places and groups, and each of the church districts had their own unique customs.

Maybe hers wasn't like the one his parents had belonged to.

Don't let a pretty smile persuade you to throw away your common sense, warned the most cautious portion of his mind. The part he took pains to listen to whenever possible. He'd learned the hard way disregarding its warnings could lead to trouble. It had whispered Chelsea Shipley was the wrong woman for him and he hadn't listened...until she'd dumped him.

"Is there something we should do to make sure the freezer keeps working?" Abby asked.

"Keep the coils cleaned and clear away any layers of ice inside the chest." He was glad to return to neutral territory where he could talk about work and not be assaulted by uncomfortable memories of what had happened fifteen years ago with Chelsea. "Don't leave the door open. Grab what you need and close it fast."

"*Gut.* Those are things we can do. *Danki* again, David, for coming today."

"It would have been a shame for the donated food to go to waste."

She laughed. "I worried, too, but realized I could have farmed out the meats to every oven in town and roasted them before they spoiled. Somehow, we would have found a way to store the meat in the refrigerators. You saved me from going door-to-door and asking to borrow an oven."

"That would have been quite the feast."

"Wouldn't it?" Her smile brightened more. "We're having a feast tonight to give thanks for how God has brought us together in Evergreen Corners. Are you and Mikayla planning to join the other teens and their parents for supper here? We'll be eating around six thirty."

How he wanted to believe the kindness in her expression! He could say yes without hesitation. Right now, Mikayla needed good people around her as she faced life without her father. It had to be devastating for her. It was for him because he'd lost his best friend, and the void left after the accident was greater than he could have imagined.

Before he could answer, Mikayla stated from the doorway, "I'm coming." She didn't put her hands on her hips as she faced him, but she might as well have.

"All right," he replied. "I'll come, too."

"You don't have to."

He translated her words to mean "I don't want you to." Not that it mattered. He wasn't going to leave her on her own with strangers.

But they weren't strangers to Mikayla. She'd been spending lots of time volunteering. He'd agreed when she'd said she wanted to help. Last night, she'd actually spoken a few words during their supper and each had been about painting inside the new houses.

That explained why her clothing was spotted bright pink. He wondered if the paint was water soluble and would wash out. He flinched. Maybe Mikayla hadn't changed much in the last ten months, but he had. Before, laundry hadn't been anything he'd thought about until he ran out of clean clothes.

Satisfied he'd agreed to attend the supper, Mikayla hurried to catch up with the two boys who were already out the door.

"Hey! Where are you going?" David called, but she didn't look at him.

Abby said, "Don't worry. They're headed to house sites to assist."

"I thought she was painting today."

"The kids pitch in wherever they're needed. They're a *gut* group of kids." She smiled again and he felt that twitch of reaction deep within him. "Mikayla has been a true blessing for us."

"I'm glad to hear that."

"In spite of what she's been through this past year, she's always ready to help others. I enjoy working with her in the kitchen." A hint of a chuckle came into her voice. "And, for a girl her age, she's an accomplished cook. You must appreciate having her be able to put a delicious meal on the table."

He was stumped on how to answer. He didn't want to admit he'd never asked Mikayla to make a meal, having promised himself she must never think he considered her a burden or a servant.

Abby's enthusiasm overwhelmed him. He wasn't accustomed to someone being so blatant with their emotions and their opinions, and he found it disconcerting. He was glad to hear Mikayla was fitting in, but to say that might reveal how little he knew about the girl.

"Six thirty for supper?" he asked to change the subject.

"*Ja*, but we'll be setting up about an hour ahead of that."

Was that an invitation or an order? David decided it would be wiser not to ask. He told her that he and Mikayla would be back later. Not waiting for her answer, he darted out of the community center so fast he didn't realize he'd left a screwdriver behind until he needed it at the shop he'd set up in an old garage next to his house.

He'd get it later, he told himself. For now, he had to get his thoughts sorted. He didn't want to be drawn into the plain world and end up wounded as his parents had been.

We were chased away by closed minds and

open mouths. As his father's words rang through his head, he had to wonder—as he hadn't before—if any of those closed minds and open mouths had been wearing a lovely smile like Abby's.

The community center looked *wunderbaar.* Even her big brother, Isaac, would have to admit Abby had taken care of every detail. Outside, snow huddled in the shadowy corners beneath trees, though it was early April, and remained in ugly gray piles on the sides of the roads. Abby had been able to convince several local volunteers to share late snowdrops and bunches of crocuses, so the tables inside were brightened by small vases filled with purple and white flowers. They offered a positive sign that spring would fill yards with daffodils, forsythias and lilacs.

A half dozen women, both plain and *Englisch*, worked in the kitchen. They dished out the vegetables, mashed potatoes and sliced meats and breads. Jenna, who was the local librarian, carried bowls of applesauce and chow-chow from the kitchen. The young woman had worked long hours to salvage materials at the library, where both the basement and ground floor had flooded. She flashed Abby a smile and a thumbs-up before turning to the refrigerator to collect more relishes to put on the tables.

The door to the street opened, allowing in cold air and an explosion of voices as teenagers and their parents arrived. Abby searched the faces. She breathed a sigh of relief when she saw Mikayla's among them.

Not only Mikayla, but David Riehl had returned. Abby hadn't been certain he would. Making sure her surprise was well hidden, she waved to the newcomers with one hand as she poured water into glasses with the other. Mikayla hung up her coat before rushing to the kitchen to help.

"No, no," Abby said with a chuckle as she put up her arm to keep the girl from going into the kitchen. "You and the other teens are *our* guests of honor tonight. Let us serve you."

"I want to help." The girl glanced at David, who was talking to one of the other *daeds*. "Please."

"Is everything all right?" Abby asked, her smile falling away.

"Everything's as it always is."

The girl's tone sent a pulse of sorrow through Abby. Mikayla seldom spoke of the car accident that had left her an orphan and had never said a word about David. Yet, the teen's grief was bubbling right beneath her too composed exterior, a volcano ready to erupt at any moment.

Abby wished she knew a way to help Mikayla to be honest with her and with her guardian. There must be some way to reach the girl.

How?

The question plagued Abby while she finished setting the tables. Her half-formed hope she could sit with the girl and David vanished when they found the last two seats at a small table with Jack and his parents. The question continued to dog her during grace, which was led by Pastor Hershey. The Mennonite minister preached at the church attached to the community center.

She ate the food that had smelled so delicious, but it had no flavor for her as ideas for helping Mikayla burst into her mind and were discarded. When the meal concluded with thick slabs of *snitz* pie, she was no closer to a solution.

Then everyone was leaving. She sought out David and Mikayla.

"*Danki* for joining us tonight," Abby said. "I'm glad you both could come. And *danki* again for your help this afternoon, David. I hope you don't have too much homework tonight, Mikayla, because you must be exhausted after helping so much this afternoon."

"Just French and English." The girl shrugged. "I speak both already, so they're easy."

Had she made a joke? If so, it was the first Abby had ever heard from her. She clamped her hands to her sides before she could fling her arms around the girl and say how delighted she was to hear humor in Mikayla's words. Glancing at David, she saw he was astonished as she was. Before she could find the right thing to say that wouldn't embarrass the teenager, they'd thanked her again and left.

Abby sighed. There had to be something she could do. *What, God?*

Knowing she must be patient because God answered prayers in His time, she turned to head into the kitchen. She was told there were enough hands to help and she'd done more than her share that day. She would have argued most days that she didn't want to leave the cleanup to others, but she was weighted with her concern for Mikayla and David. Going home to seek God's guidance might be the best thing she could do.

Reece held the door open for her after she'd put on her black coat and tied her black bonnet over her *kapp*. The teenager fell into step with her as they walked up the hill along the village green.

"My folks needed to head over the mountain

to pick up my sister," he said when Abby asked why he was walking home instead of going with his parents. "They had to slip out before dessert because her math tutor gets annoyed if they're late picking her up."

"There was extra pie. You could have—"

He held up a grocery bag she hadn't noticed and grinned in the thin glow from the streetlight. "Already taken care of. Enough for them and for my sister."

"And for you?"

"Yep." He chuckled. "I didn't want them to eat alone."

"You're a *gut* son."

"It's good pie."

Abby laughed along with him. It'd taken some of the teens a little time to get accustomed to being around plain volunteers, but, once they'd realized the Amish weren't going to chide them for every action or expect them to be serious every minute, they'd relaxed and treated her and the others like the rest of the adult volunteers. With respect and the assumption their elders were out of touch. She remembered feeling the same way when she'd turned thirteen and known she'd be finished with school in a little over a year.

They were a block from where she lived in an apartment over the mayor's garage when a dark-colored car raced over the top of the hill and squealed to a stop not far from them. Reece tensed beside her as both windows on the driver's side rolled down. Seeing several teens, at least one of them a girl, in the car, she wondered what they wanted.

"Hey, Maddox, going for an older woman now?" Laughter burst from the car. "You going to grow one of those beards to impress your Aymish girlfriend?" They pronounced the word with a long *a*. More rude laughter was followed by smacking sounds as if they were trying to kiss something as huge as an elephant.

When a teen made a comment about his sister, Reece put down the bag with the pie and took a step toward the car.

Abby grabbed his arm, halting him. She hid her grip from the kids who rained taunts on him. They mustn't guess she was keeping him from stepping into their snare. There were at least four kids in the vehicle and they'd let Reece take the first swing before they pummeled him.

"*Danki* for your comments," she said as she picked up the bag and handed it to Reece.

He looked from it to her, but she said nothing. Instead she continued along the steep sidewalk at a slow pace that would look as if she didn't have a care in the world. As she passed the car, the teens exchanged glances as if they couldn't believe what they were hearing. *Gut!* Giving them pause might allow them time to realize they were acting like *dummkopfs*.

Suddenly the car peeled out as another vehicle came up the hill. She guessed they didn't want to be seen. They went down the street too fast and skidded with a squeal around the corner.

Beside her, Reece let out his breath in a sigh. She patted his arm in silent commiseration, but tensed when the red truck came to a stop beside them. What now?

She got the answer when the driver stepped out and called, "Were those kids bothering you?" David's voice was laced with anger.

"We're fine." Abby pointed at the bag Reece carried. "The pie is fine."

"Abby?" Both David and Mikayla, who'd stepped out of the passenger's side, gasped her name at the same time.

Mikayla rushed to Reece, who was shaking with residual emotion. He nodded to her, but spoke to Abby. "I thought I'd make sure you got home okay." He knocked his work boot against the pile of refrozen snow mixed with last fall's leaves. "I didn't think I'd have you saving the day for me."

"Will that cause more trouble for you?" she asked.

He shook his head. "Nothing can cause *more*

trouble for us with those guys and their girls. They're bullies, and they harass everyone."

"Everyone?" David joined them on the sidewalk.

Reece faltered, then said, "Yeah, everyone."

"And nobody does anything about it?"

"We ignore them. The Bible says not to speak evil of someone else, so we're trying to ignore their words. We know they aren't true." He glanced at Abby. "At least, we try to ignore them."

"And you're doing a *gut* job." She patted his arm. "You'd better get that pie home before your family wonders if we've kept you washing dishes."

He nodded and headed up the street with Mikayla matching his steps. The two teens spoke softly, so Abby couldn't guess what they were saying.

"Are you sure you're okay?" David asked as he watched the two kids moving together from shadow to lamplight.

"I'm fine, and Reece will be. He knows well-aimed cruel words can hurt, but they're words spoken by people he doesn't respect."

"Bullies start with words, Abby. When those don't get them what they want, they turn to other means."

"I know. That's why I'm going to urge the

kids to stick together." She hesitated and then asked, "Would you drive Reece home? I don't like to think of those other kids finding him by himself."

"No need. His house is there." He pointed to the top of the hill. "I'll wait and make sure he gets home. I'll give them a few minutes. Then I'll pick up Mikayla."

"That's a *gut* idea. I think Reece needs someone his own age to talk to right now."

"You've got real insight into these kids, don't you?"

"I try. If you see something else I can do better, let me know."

"I will," he replied, but he didn't look at her.

She fought not to frown. David had avoided her eyes several times this afternoon. Now he was doing the same. What was he trying to hide? His life had been turned inside out by becoming the *daed* to a teenager. Maybe both he and Mikayla needed guidance to ease into their new lives.

She would be glad to help. But how? She hoped God would show her the way.

Chapter Three

"Abby, are you here?"

Looking up from the menu she was preparing for the coming week, Abby glanced at the clock in the community center kitchen. It was nearly 10:00 a.m. Where had the morning gone?

She smiled as Beth Ann Overholt walked into the kitchen. The dark-haired midwife volunteered when she could in Evergreen Corners. With her practice in Lancaster County, Pennsylvania, she had to find times—two weeks each visit—to help with the rebuilding. She was much taller than Abby and wore a brace on her right leg. Like Abby, she dressed plainly, but her *kapp* was pleated as befitted her life as a Mennonite.

For a moment, Abby considered asking Beth Ann's advice on how to help David and Mikayla. She'd been pondering the question for the past week and didn't have an answer. She guessed that because most of Beth Ann's interactions were at births, she wouldn't have much more insight than Abby did into teenagers.

"I'm right where I always am at this time of day," Abby replied as she motioned for her friend to come over to the table. "Getting ready for the midday meal and trying to come up with menus based on what we've got in the freezer. It looks as if we'll be having venison burgers a lot in the near future."

"All right by me."

"You'll eat anything put in front of you."

"Hard work makes a girl hungry."

"I can't argue with that." Abby laughed as she put down the paper and pencil. "A cup of *kaffi*?"

"Yes, but I'll have to take it to go. We're supposed to finish the painting at the McGoverns' house today."

"Then let me get you enough cups for the whole crew. How many?"

"Five. Do you have disposable cups?"

"Thanks to the generosity of Spezio's market, we do." The grocery store, situated at the edge of town, had been cut off from many residents for more than three months. Everyone had been pleased when that route out of Evergreen Corners had been opened to traffic again. "I don't know what we'd do if they didn't keep us supplied with paper goods."

Beth Ann chuckled. "You'd figure out some other way to get by." She scanned the kitchen while Abby went to the pantry and lifted out a stack of insulated cups. "Are you alone here today?"

"*Ja.* That nasty cold has half the town in bed and the other half trying to avoid catching it."

"I know. That's why we've only got five on the painting crew today."

Abby poured *kaffi* from the big urn and set packets of creamer and sugar onto one of the trays used to transport drinks to the various building and work sites. "We need to contact Isaac to see if anyone up north can come down for a few days."

"That's already been done." Beth Ann hefted the tray. "I heard someone over at the high school saying your brother will have more volunteers here by the end of the week."

"I'm glad to hear that."

"Thanks, Abby." She turned to go, then paused. "Oh… I almost forgot the reason I came by. Glen wants to see you."

Glen Landis was the project manager for the rebuilding in Evergreen Corners. He worked for a Mennonite organization but coordinated with Amish Helping Hands and other groups who'd sent volunteers and supplies to help. As well, he kept each project on schedule by making sure building materials were ready when the crews needed them. Handling any disputes was also part of his job, and he did it so well Abby had heard of only one instance where there had been a major disagreement.

He was the busiest man in town. Maybe in the whole state, and Abby knew his time was precious. If he wanted to see her, it must be for something important.

"When?" she asked.

"Now." Beth Ann gave her a guilty grin. "I was supposed to deliver the message an hour ago, but I got waylaid when I was recruited to help unload a truck of donated furniture. I must have carried two dozen lamps into the town barn. People can come and pick out what they want once their houses are repaired." Rolling her eyes as if she were no older than the teen volunteers, she said, "Look! I'm delaying you again, and the coffee is getting cold."

"Sounds like I don't have any time to waste, do I?" Abby followed the other woman to the door. Grabbing her coat and black bonnet, she closed the door.

Beth Ann strode away toward the center of town, but Abby lingered for a moment to draw in a deep breath of the fresh air that was flavored by mud and the aroma of freshly cut lumber. It'd been close to freezing when she'd come to work before dawn. Now the sunshine was making the snow dwindle into puddles.

She smiled when her feet sank into the damp earth as she crossed the village green. The faint color of new grass was visible beneath the brown remnants from last fall. Without snow, the damaged gazebo appeared more rickety. That project must wait until homes and businesses were safe and repaired.

And then she would need to leave Evergreen Corners. She didn't like to think about that. In the small town, she'd found many ways to help. At home, her older brother would have everything under control, as he always did. There wouldn't be anything for her to do, he'd tell her as he had so often, other than to find a husband and set up a household of her own.

Abby didn't realize she'd been stamping her feet with the intensity of her thoughts until the heel of her boot got stuck. She wiggled it free and rushed toward the sidewalk as she forced herself to calm down. Isaac believed the only way she could find happiness was to marry.

She didn't have anything against marriage. In fact, she dreamed of becoming the wife of a man who loved her, but she didn't trust her heart. The last time she'd listened to it, putting her own yearnings first, tragedy had followed. A shiver rushed along her spine when the memories of that night almost nine years ago exploded. Instead of being there for Bert, a troubled young man she'd known needed help, she'd thought of spending time with Wilmer, who'd caught her eye and made her heart beat faster. Her heart had betrayed her, because Bert might not have been injured in an accident when he challenged Wilmer to a buggy race. At the time they'd lined up their buggies, she'd been asleep, never knowing about the drama playing out along the road not far from her family's farm. She hadn't imagined what could happen and how her name and reputation would become synonymous with the accident.

Since that night, when she'd joined others praying Bert wouldn't die, and during the long months of his recovery and Wilmer's trial afterward, she'd promised herself and God she wouldn't let her desires come before anyone else's. She would focus on helping with her family's move to Vermont two years ago as well as volunteering to work with Amish Helping Hands. That had kept her too busy for walking out with a young man, especially the *wrong* young man. Not that she'd ever met anyone who made her think of walking out together.

Except David Riehl.

She silenced that thought as she reached for the door in one wing of the high school. David was an *Englischer* with no time for walking out, either. What did she know about him other than he was struggling to be the *daed* to a teenager?

Not giving herself a chance to answer, Abby went into the school. She stopped at the office to let them know she had a meeting with Glen and then half ran to his office, knowing she was late.

She knocked on the door with its frosted glass and heard the call for her to come in. As she'd expected, Glen sat behind a cluttered desk in what had been a classroom in the high school. For the past five months, it had served as an office for the project manager who oversaw the volunteers and vendors together with the families who were having their homes rebuilt. Calendars listing when supplies should be ordered and when they'd be delivered vied for space along the walls with house plans. Samples of flooring and cabinet doors were stacked in one corner while cases of light bulbs leaned at a precarious angle against another.

"Come in, Abby!" he said as a greeting when he stood. His kind face was lined with more wrinkles daily. "We've just started."

We?

In astonishment, she saw the man who'd been filling her thoughts rising from a straight chair across the desk from Glen. She almost demanded to know why David was part of the meeting, then bit back the words. She was there to help, not cause friction.

"Danki," she said when David cleared another chair of stacks of paper so she'd have a place to sit.

Folding her hands on her lap, Abby waited for Glen to speak. She didn't have to wait long.

As he sat, pulling his chair in closer to his desk, the project manager said, "You may have heard I wasn't in favor of having youth volunteers when it was first suggested to me."

Abby nodded. Michael Miller, an Amish volunteer who'd decided to remain in Evergreen Corners in the hope of building a church district in the town, had first suggested having the teens help. Once he was baptized, he would marry and share with his family one of the new houses set far enough from the brook that they shouldn't be flooded again. The mayor had hired him to build new shelves in the library, but that project had been put on hold. So, for now, he'd kept working with the house crews, using his skills as a fine carpenter to piece together moldings and window frames.

"You've changed your mind," David said.

"Completely. I've talked with the supervisors at each building site, and they agree with me."

"Agree about what?" Abby asked.

"That we need to make our teens into a cohesive group that works together while enjoying the special fellowship they would experience if they weren't volunteering so many hours. We're developing a program to balance their volunteer hours and their homework hours and allow them time for socializing with each other. We want, as well, to include faith lessons as part of the program." Glen leaned forward and folded his arms on his desk. When papers crunched under his elbows, he grimaced. He moved the offending papers and then refolded his arms on the empty blotter. "We want to give them the tools they need to deal with the challenges they're facing right now."

"So you've heard about the bullying, too?" Abby couldn't see any reason not to be blunt.

He nodded, his expression grim. "We would like to think when someone sees a gathering of brothers and sisters toiling in God's name, that sight should inspire love. Unfortunately, some young people prefer to belittle our volunteers."

"Talking to the bullies' parents—"

"Has obtained us promises they'll speak with their children. Some of the bullies have stopped. A couple have inquired about helping us. However, a core of about five teens have continued to be disruptive."

"What can I do to help?" Abby asked.

David cut his eyes toward her as he corrected, "What can *we* do to help?"

"That's what I meant," she hurried to add.

He looked away, but this time he wasn't hiding anything from her. He was irritated at her choice of words. She hadn't wanted to speak for anyone but herself. He should know that. With a start, she realized—again—she had no idea what he should know because she didn't know him.

"I'm glad to hear both of you are eager to get this program going," Glen said with a broadening smile. "We need two adult coordinators to develop our program and work with the kids on a two-to three-times-a-week basis. Will you be willing to get us started?"

"*Ja*, of course, we will." Abby stiffened. She should have thought before she blurted her answer because she was committing David to something he might not want to do. He had a lot on his plate with Mikayla and his repair business.

However, working with the teens could be the best way for her to help David and Mikayla grow closer. They'd been brought together by tragedy, but they needed to believe God wanted them to have joy and love in their lives. Could David see that? She must not push too hard because she'd already learned both David and Mikayla were stubborn. Being subtle when she could help people wasn't her strong point, but she must try.

"I mean," she added, hoping she hadn't already messed up this opportunity to help David and Mikayla and the other teens, "*I* am willing to help with this program."

"Good." Glen turned to focus on the man sitting beside her. "And what about you, David?"

She gasped. She hadn't intended to put David in the hot seat and she hoped he'd see the needs of his family as she did. If he didn't... No, she didn't want to think her hopes had been dashed before they'd come to life.

David didn't have to look at Abby to know she was sorry for having spoken out of turn again. First, she'd acted as if she didn't want to work with him; next, she was volunteering him without asking if he was interested. He'd heard her quick intake of breath in the silence following the calm question Glen had posed to him.

Every instinct told him to jump to his feet and tell Glen he had the wrong guy. If David agreed to this idea, he—and Mikayla—would be spending more time with the Amish volunteers.

Mikayla already talked about Abby almost

every time she opened her mouth. His daughter didn't need to spend *more* time with her. Mikayla would want to be part of the program, and the one way he could be certain she didn't put herself in a position to be hurt as his parents had been was to be there to keep an eye on her.

He wasn't sure how he was going to find the time with the work he had lined up, but he'd vowed at Boyd's funeral to take care of Mikayla as if she were his own flesh and blood. Somehow, he'd figure out what to do. He'd go over his schedule to find pockets of time to spend with the teens.

Knowing what he must do didn't halt him from being cautious enough to say, "I like this idea, Glen, but I think Abby and I need some time to talk about how we would handle this."

Abby looked at him in astonishment. Did she always jump off a cliff without bothering to see how deep the chasm was?

He couldn't do that. He had to consider each of the alternatives in the hope of seeing a solution instead of getting tangled up in his emotions. That was the way to deal with problems. He looked at his hands spread across his knees. His knuckles were pale from where he'd been gripping his legs.

"I can give you a couple of days," Glen replied. "No more. The bullying seems to be getting worse. I want to, as they used to say in the old movies, head the problem off at the pass. I can't think of anyone better to do the job than you two." He relaxed and smiled. "To tell you the truth, I asked around for recommendations, and your names were the ones I heard over and over. Abby, you've done a tremendous job with the teens and, David, the word around Evergreen Corners is you can fix anything."

David smiled wryly. "I don't know if people meant I could put an end to bullying. It's not like finding the right part and installing it."

"I think it is," Abby said. "We need to figure out what's bothering those youngsters and help them."

"We're not talking about Amish kids here." He tried to keep his annoyance out of his voice. "Your kids may be well behaved but—"

Her laugh halted him. "Our *kinder* can be as badly behaved as *Englisch* ones." She grew serious. "I know *Englischers* like to think we're different because of what we wear and how we try to live our lives as close as we can to Jesus's teachings, but we're human beings. Everyone makes mistakes, and we hope we can learn from those. Most important, we learn to offer forgiveness and accept it."

He wanted to say that wasn't the experience his family had, but talking about the past wouldn't help deal with the future. "Look, we need to talk about this, and I'm sure Glen has other things to do than to listen to us."

The project manager gave them a grin as he patted a stack of papers almost eight inches high. "These have to be handled before I can hit the hay tonight. So talk it over when you have a chance and get back to me in two days. I'd like to be able to give you longer, but I can't. We need to deal with this before it becomes a crisis."

David stood and watched as Abby did, every motion she made graceful. As he turned to leave, Glen called his name.

He turned. "Something else?"

"I wanted to let you know we'll be deciding in the next month whose three houses we're going to build next."

"Good." He was too aware of Abby listening, so he didn't give Glen a chance to say more before he walked out of the room. Aware of Abby following him down the hallway to the office, he waited for her to sign out after he had. He held the outside door open for her.

She paused on the sidewalk and faced him. "Are you going to be working on the next houses?"

"I lend a hand now and then when I can."

The answer seemed to satisfy her because she

asked, "Do you have time for a cup of *kaffi*?" A warm flush climbed her cheeks, brightening them until they matched the soft pink shade of her dress. "I mean, coffee."

He smiled. "What you said was close enough to English so I could figure it out. Yes, I think having a chat is a good idea."

"Let's go to the diner." Twin dimples emphasized her smile. "I've been curious what it looks like now, and they should have the windows open on the sunporch so we can enjoy this beautiful day." She must have misread his hesitation because she added, "My treat."

He forced any hints of surprise from his face. He'd heard his father complain that the Amish were so frugal they wouldn't spend a penny unless absolutely necessary. Abby was offering to pay the tab. Though it wasn't for more than a cup of coffee, her easy offer contradicted what he'd assumed was true.

Had he misunderstood his father? He couldn't keep from wondering if she were unique among the plain people or if he, like his daughter, was setting his new family up for trouble.

In either case, the only way he would know for certain was to spend as much time with her as Mikayla did, so his daughter wouldn't be blindsided and hurt.

Chapter Four

Della's Diner was at the center of Evergreen Corners, just west of the bridge crossing Washboard Brook that bisected the village. It faced a huge mill building that had been converted to artists' lofts. Most studios on the lower two floors had been damaged during the flood. The building's foundation had been undermined, so nobody could go inside until the stone was replaced by concrete.

The diner had been half stripped away by the rushing water, but its owners had shored it up as soon as the brook began to recede. It had reopened three weeks ago.

David wondered what had changed inside and was surprised to see not much had. The light green walls glistened with fresh paint. They were covered with new pictures of chickens and roosters as well as knickknacks sitting on open shelving in the place of the old pictures and bric-a-brac that had washed away. Everywhere he looked there was poultry of various colors from traditional to a steampunk rooster set next to the cash register. That rooster was made out of bright purple metal with faucet handles for eyes and webbed feet like a goose. He was amazed the owners had found so many items to replace the lost ones.

A few patrons sat at the counter running along one wall toward a swinging door to the kitchen. Pies topped with generous amounts of meringue were displayed in tiered glass cases set not far from the coffeepots giving off an enticing aroma.

A middle-aged waitress came forward to greet them. Her astonishment when she glanced at Abby was quickly hidden behind her professional smile.

He had thought, by now, the residents of Evergreen Corners would be accustomed to seeing plain people. He almost laughed. Not a ha-ha laugh, but an ironic one. He'd stared the same way himself when he'd realized Mikayla's Abby was Amish.

The waitress held a pair of menus. "Inside or on the sunporch?"

"Sunporch," David said, thinking of how Abby had mentioned sitting by an open window.

Abby had noticed Glen's comments as they were leaving, but seemed to believe that Glen had been asking for his help. Letting her think that meant he didn't have to answer questions— as he had for FEMA personnel and Boyd's private insurance company—about the house where Boyd had raised his daughter. It'd been destroyed in the flood during Hurricane Kevin last fall. If Mikayla hadn't been living with David, she could have been lost in the storm. He hadn't spoken of that to anyone, but it tainted his dreams night after night.

"This way." The waitress aimed another glance, one she must have figured was too surreptitious for anybody to notice, at Abby before leading the way through a broad doorway to the diner's other room.

If Abby noticed the waitress's gawking, she gave no sign. Was she used to people staring? She might be too polite to acknowledge them. Or maybe—and he was astonished how much he wished this was true—she hadn't seen the waitress's looks in her direction.

He was shocked at the sense of protectiveness surging through him. Not because he wanted to make sure his daughter wasn't hurt again. This time, he longed to shield Abby from being wounded by a rude look in her direction. Shocked by his reaction, he pushed it aside and focused on following the two women onto the sunporch.

A row of windows lined one wall and the others were decorated with more chickens. A couple of televisions hung near the ceiling and were on but muted. Both were showing weather maps of the Midwest with areas marked in red for strong storms.

The waitress led them to a table next to a window. As he glanced out, he noticed the brook was much higher than it'd been a few days ago. Snow on the mountains flanking the valley must be thawing fast. The water was a pale brown with mud, and white foam marked the large boulders. Even with the spring melt, the brook remained below its banks.

David took the seat across from where Abby sat and smiled his thanks when the waitress handed them each a menu and hurried away to seat other patrons.

"What's tasty?" Abby asked.

He hesitated, aware she'd offered to pay for their tab. "The coffee's good."

"I saw those pies on the counter. Don't you think we need to try some? A friend of mine makes them, so I'm sure they're delicious."

Though he was curious which of her friends baked the pies, he didn't want to pry. Better to keep his distance on any personal matter when dealing with the plain folk. He'd learned that from his folks, though they'd never used those exact words. Instead he'd listened to what they *hadn't* said about their lives as Amish.

When the waitress returned to the table, Abby ordered a cup of coffee and a piece of strawberry-rhubarb pie. He asked for coffee as well as chocolate-cream pie. He could see that pleased Abby. Now that he'd volunteered to work with her, he should get to know her better, so he could discover what strengths she had to offer as well as any ideas. He wanted to get their project started. The sooner begun, the sooner finished.

Or at least he hoped so.

"So were you born and raised in Evergreen Corners?" Abby asked after two cups were set on the table.

"I moved here before I started school." He stirred sugar into his cup. "I've lived here long enough that everyone accepts me as a native."

"What made you decide to be a repairman?"

"I like using tools and figuring out puzzles, so it seemed an obvious step to fix broken appliances." He waited until plates topped by generous slabs of pie were set between them. After he thanked the waitress, he asked Abby, "Do you always ask people you work with questions?"

Her smile looked far more genuine than his had felt. "I ask everyone questions. How else can I learn about people if I don't ask? I know you're Mikayla's guardian and you're concerned about her and her friends. That's it."

"I know you like to cook and you're Amish." He didn't add how often his daughter spoke her name...on the few occasions when Mikayla talked.

"I don't enjoy cooking that much. What I love is baking." She took a bite of her pie. "Though I don't think I've ever baked anything as delicious as this."

He didn't respond as he might have with anyone else. His parents had often told him how plain people disdained bragging about themselves or others.

Instead he said the obvious. "Glen wants us to work together with the kids."

"Ja." Faint pink brightened her cheeks. "I'm sorry if I forced you to accept the assignment."

"You didn't force me. I want to help the kids deal with these bullies."

"Has it been going on long?"

"The bullying?" He took a drink of coffee, savoring its flavor while he thought about when he'd first heard rumors of the bullies. "About three to four months, as far as I know."

She leaned back in her chair and looked out the window, offering him a view of her profile.

Her chin might be a bit too assertive, but her face was lovely from any angle.

Taking another gulp of coffee, he silenced the thought. He shouldn't be thinking about anything but trying to convince Mikayla that they were family. And he shouldn't be admiring the Amish woman sitting on the other side of the table. What irony that the first woman who'd caught his attention in years lived the life his parents disdained.

"I wonder," she mused, "if the bullying has anything to do with the tragedies inflicting Evergreen Corners."

"I don't see any reason how or why."

"And I can't see any reason how or why not."

He arched his brows. "You're beginning to sound like a true Vermonter."

"Really?"

"Vermonters enjoy being contrary, or so we're told." He folded his arms on top of the checkered tablecloth. "There's one thing we agree on. The weather is and always will be the most important topic."

She laughed. "It is for farmers."

"And everyone else. What the weather was, what it will be, when it'll rain, when it'll snow."

She laughed. "I haven't been in Vermont long, but I know the saying. 'If you don't like the weather—'"

"'Wait a minute and it'll change,'" he said in unison with her.

A hand clapped on his shoulder and David looked up at a thin, rangy man whose blond hair was laced with silver. "Jens, how are you?"

"Doing great. You?" Jens's eyes cut toward Abby.

"Jens, this is Abby Kauffman. Abby, this is Jens Gundersen. You know his son, Jack."

She smiled. "So nice to meet you. You have a *wunderbaar* son. He's always willing to pitch in."

"I'm glad to hear that, Ms. Kauffman."

"Abby, please." She motioned toward an empty chair. "Would you like to join us?"

"Thanks, but I dropped in to get some coffee to go." He gave them a jaunty wave. "If my boy gives you any trouble, Abby, let me know."

"I would if he was a problem, but he isn't. You're raising a *gut* kid."

Jens was grinning with pride as he walked over to where a large cup was waiting for him by the register.

A storm of unexpected sensations rushed through David, too many to identify as each fought for dominance. Except for one.

Confusion.

He was confused by the contrast between what he knew about the Amish and how Abby acted. She was the epitome of kindness and generosity, the complete opposite of how his parents described the plain people. Somehow, he was going to have to figure her out before he—and Mikayla—could be wounded as his father and mother had been by trusting the Amish.

Abby thanked the waitress for refilling her cup. As she stirred more milk into her *kaffi*, she listened as yet another person stopped to speak with David. She'd been sitting with him for almost a half hour and they had yet to discuss any ideas for working with the volunteer teens. People paused by the table for various reasons. Some wanted to say hi. A few had questions about work they wanted him to do. Others were simply curious why he was at the diner with an Amish woman.

She smiled when he introduced her to each person, but was aware of time passing without anything getting done. She couldn't linger too much longer because she needed to get tonight's supper started.

Drawing in a deep breath as David spoke to the mayor's husband, she gazed out the window. She could hear the brook murmur to itself.

"Fascinating, isn't it?" asked David, startling her because she hadn't realized he'd finished his conversation.

"*Ja*. Peaceful and beautiful, though I know it wasn't during the flood." She leaned closer to the cool glass. "I wonder if the brook feels bad about the damage it's done."

"That's a fanciful thought."

She smiled at him. "And *fanciful* is a fancy word."

"Something you're not allowed to say?" he asked with unexpected heat.

Her brows lowered and her grin fell away. "The only things we're proscribed from saying are listed in the Bible. Not taking the Lord's name in vain, for example."

"I assumed that."

"But you assumed there were other things we aren't allowed to say because we're Amish."

A hint of a flush climbed from beneath his collar. Was he embarrassed by what he'd said? She couldn't help recalling other comments he'd made suggesting he had no use for plain people. That didn't make sense. He'd been nice to her and he hadn't kept Mikayla from working with her and other plain volunteers. *Ja*, he'd hesitated when Glen had asked him to work with Abby, but she didn't think that was because she was Amish.

Could she have been wrong? Did he have an objection to being around Amish people?

If so, she wasn't helping matters by being

confrontational. So many verses in the Bible spoke of the importance of gently teaching those who needed to learn.

"Now I need to apologize," she said. "Talking to people is the best way to find out more about them. That's what my *grossdawdi* always said." Heat surged up her own face. "I mean, my grandfather. I need to remember you don't speak our language."

"German, right?"

"*Ja*, but it's not quite the same as the language spoken in Germany. More of a dialect. We call it *Deitsch*." She smiled, hoping her expression would lessen the tension between them. "So what do you say to getting to know each other while we hammer out what we're going to do for the teens?"

"You like to help others, don't you?"

"*Ja*." She picked up a forkful of pie but didn't taste it as she asked, "What about you? You must be willing to help others if you took Mikayla into your home after the accident."

"I was surprised to find myself appointed as her guardian by Boyd's will." He stared down at his *kaffi* as if he'd never seen it before. "I don't know why he chose me."

"Maybe because he knew you'd give his daughter a *gut* home."

"Maybe. I don't know. I never had a chance

to ask. All I know is Boyd depended on me to take care of his daughter."

"And you don't want to let him down?"

"No." He took a drink and shifted his eyes away.

Abby chided herself for bringing up the subject. From what she'd been told by Mikayla's friends, Boyd St. Pierre had died less than a year ago. Her words, though she meant them to be comforting, might be like picking at a barely healed scar.

"Let's talk about the program for the teens," she said.

"You make it sound as if there's something already in place. Don't we have to start this from scratch?"

"*Ja*, but I don't think Glen expects us to do anything structured. It sounded to me like he wants us to spend time with the kids and help them discover tools to protect them from these bullies. We can combine fun with lessons about living with God."

"Don't take this the wrong way, but some of the parents might not want their kids being taught by someone who's Amish." Again, his eyes didn't meet hers.

Was he one of the parents who'd be upset if a plain person spoke of following God through life? She should ask, but didn't. Putting him into a more unpleasant position wasn't going to help them complete the task Glen had given them.

"Most of our teen volunteers attend services at the Mennonite chapel. Let's speak with Pastor Hershey."

"I can do that."

"Danki."

"You're welcome."

She waited for him to say something else, but silence grew between them. Sounds came from other diners and the traffic passing in front of the building. David looked everywhere but at her. She didn't need a sign on his forehead announcing he'd rather be somewhere else.

"David," she said as she pushed her plate and cup aside, "if you don't want to work on this project, say so. I know you're busy with your job and with Mikayla. I understand, and I'm sure Glen will, too."

"No, I said I'll help, and I don't renege on my promises."

"No one would think less of you if—"

"Thank you, Abby, but I don't need you offering me platitudes and convenient excuses." Her shock at his icy words must have been visible on her face because he apologized.

She waved aside his words. *"Danki."* Again, she felt her cheeks grow warm. "I'm sorry. I mean, thank you."

"I got that. The words sound pretty much the same. Let's start our work together with our first rule."

"What's that?"

"Honesty. If I don't understand something you say, I'll ask you. You do the same with me."

"I like that rule."

"Good. Now, what should be our next rule?"

"We make this fun for the teens and for ourselves. If we act as if this is drudgery, the kids will sense it and we'll lose our chance to help them."

"Fun?" He arched his brows as if responding to something he'd heard in his head, then sighed. "That may be harder for me to follow than the first rule. Nobody's ever described me as fun. In fact, the opposite."

"Well, then, we'll have to see how we can change that, ain't so?"

He gave her the faintest grin, but she took it as a victory. As they continued to talk about possible activities for the youngsters, she couldn't doubt he cared about his daughter and her friends. He was a man of strong emotions, though he tried to hide that fact. She couldn't help wondering why.

Chapter Five

Giving the kitchen floor one last swish with the mop, Abby bent to pick up the bucket of filthy water. She or one of the other volunteers mopped the floor at least once a day, but it never seemed clean.

She couldn't get rid of the dirt and she couldn't get rid of the feeling there was more than David had explained to his assertion last week that he wasn't someone others believed liked to have fun. Who had accused him of that and why?

She flinched. Accusations weren't always based on truth. She knew that too well. When she'd accepted Wilmer's offer to take her home in his buggy, she'd never anticipated she'd be blamed for a horrible accident later that night when he and Bert decided to race their buggies. The whispers that had followed were filled with half-truths, and she'd learned her attempts to correct the rumors added fuel to their speed along the Amish grapevine.

Looking around the kitchen, she sighed. She'd been silly to think she could leave the past behind in Pennsylvania. Maybe David was wiser than she was because he hadn't tried to do the same. Instead he'd remained in Evergreen Corners, making a life for himself and now for Mikayla. He'd accepted himself as he was and moved forward.

As she'd been trying to do.

Abby finished cleaning the kitchen. The other volunteers would be arriving to begin preparations for the evening meal. According to the schedule posted on the refrigerator with a magnet, tonight was supposed to be hamburgers and french fries.

After she'd put the cleaning supplies away, she checked to make sure there were plenty of potatoes. Fries were a favorite, and she'd learned to make extra because no matter how many were prepared, every morsel would be gone by the time the volunteers rose from the tables.

There were enough potatoes for the evening's meal, but the pantry needed to be resupplied. She made a list of the items for next week and set the list on a counter while she tied on her black bonnet and pulled on her wool coat, which was the same color.

A chill clung to the wind, but the sunshine was bright on the purple crocus buds between the sidewalk and the building. They wobbled, top-heavy, as they waited for the perfect moment to burst into welcome bits of color.

A shadow crossed the sidewalk in front of her. Looking up, she grinned.

"Isaac!" She gave her older brother a big hug. His black hat was askew on his light brown hair that the sun bleached with blond streaks every spring. More than ten years her senior, he remained clean-shaved because he'd never wedded.

Her older brother was, like David, not someone who displayed his feelings. Not that it was necessary. Isaac loved her as much as he did the rest of their family, which were the center of his world. When he wasn't in Evergreen Corners, he spent long hours working on their farm in northeastern Vermont. He would never inherit the farm—it would go to their youngest brother, Herman—but Isaac was the best dairyman in the family and he'd taken on the responsibility of passing along his skills to their other brothers. He'd been scouting farms for when he was ready to marry and start a home and a herd of his own.

Not bothering to hide her grin when she saw the paper bag he used as a suitcase, she asked, "How long can you stay this time?"

He motioned for her to lead the way up the street toward her apartment over the mayor's garage, he replied, "At least a few weeks. I want to be back before the next group of calves is born."

"You've got to learn to trust Herman." She always teased him about his overprotectiveness of their brothers. "One of these days, he'll have to handle a birth on his own."

Isaac grumbled as he stepped around a pile of unmelted snow. "When he's ready, but that's not now."

Knowing by his tone Isaac was worried about the calving, she said, "Your room is just as you left it." She gave him a teasing smile. "Except you've got clean sheets on your bed and no dirty towels in the hamper."

"You didn't need to change the sheets. I'd slept on them only a couple of nights last time I was here."

"You're my brother. Until we find some woman silly enough to marry you, I need to make sure you have a decent meal to eat and fresh linen to sleep on after a long day of work."

He smiled. "Are you saying I should be looking for a wife because you've found yourself a husband?"

"Who's here for me to marry?" She ignored the abrupt image of David's handsome face in her mind. She hardly knew him, and he was *Englisch*. "All the plain men here are married." She grinned. "However, there are several women who aren't."

"No matchmaking, little sister."

"I'll agree to no matchmaking in Evergreen Corners if you will."

He nodded. "You're right. We're here to help others, not to look for spouses."

As they reached a white Colonial with dark green shutters, a woman burst out of the house. Gladys Whittaker was mayor of Evergreen Corners, and she was talking on her cell phone every time Abby saw her. The mayor's neat, bright blue suit reminded Abby how her own dress and apron were covered with stains from making the midday meal. She and Isaac stopped to let the mayor rush past them.

Gladys looked over her shoulder to say, "Good to see you, Isaac." She didn't add more as her phone began beeping and making other odd sounds.

Abby said a quick prayer for Gladys Whittaker. The mayor worked with national and state emergency management agencies on flood recovery. While Glen coordinated the volunteers, she handled everything else with the tiny staff at the village hall. The first floor of the building had been flooded, but as the brook rose, many of the records had been rushed upstairs by the mayor, her husband and the village clerk. They'd spent a perilous night stuck in the village hall, which had struggled to hold against the raging waters. It had given Gladys and the others a bird's-eye view of other buildings being destroyed.

"How are you doing, Gladys?" Isaac asked when the mayor frowned at her phone.

"Looking for my mind, which I lost when I agreed to run for mayor."

Abby smiled. Her brother always asked the mayor about herself, and she always gave him the same answer.

"Did you bring other volunteers with you?" Gladys asked. "I hope so. We aren't blessed with many as dedicated as the Kauffmans."

"I brought four volunteers. They're with Glen getting their assignments for work and where to sleep. All men, though two are sixteen."

"The younger ones should join the group Abby is overseeing with one of our parents."

Isaac gave his sister a curious glance, but she didn't explain. That could wait until he dropped off the few things he'd brought with him. She'd leave the account of how she and David had agreed to help with the teenagers until later.

Abby followed her brother up the outside stairs along the side of the garage. Going into the tiny apartment, she waited in the cramped kitchen while he took his bag into the larger of the two bedrooms. She chuckled her breath. *Larger* was a silly way to describe a bedroom with space for a twin bed and a dresser. Her room didn't have a dresser, but she'd found cardboard boxes to store her things in the tiny closet.

He didn't say anything to her as they walked down the stairs. She guessed her brother was eager to get to work and wouldn't ask her more about the teen group now.

He confirmed that when he said, "I need to head over to the school. Glen told me before I left to let him know when I returned to Evergreen Corners."

Abby wasn't surprised. Isaac had extraordinary skills as a mason, and he had overseen setting up the forms for each new house's foundation as well as supervising pouring the concrete. There never was any question if his calculations were right or his corners square. He laid out the foundation by hand, using a laser only to confirm what he'd done. Not once had the forms needed adjustment.

"I was heading that way myself," she said. Fishing the slip of paper from her pocket, she smiled. "Could you give Glen this list of the supplies we need for the community center?"

He nodded and took the wrinkled page. Glancing at it, he grimaced. "I'm glad I'm not working in the kitchen. One hundred pounds of onions? I wouldn't want to peel and chop those."

"I hope the weather is warm enough we can open the windows soon. I'm tired of onion tears." She started to add more, then noticed a familiar silhouette coming toward them out of the brilliant sunshine.

David's easy gait made short work of the distance between them. He wore a bright yellow knit hat with green stripes along with his black puffy coat. Thick gloves covered his hands. His eyes narrowed when his gaze alighted on her brother, but his smile didn't waver.

"David, this is my brother Isaac Kauffman," Abby said, hoping she sounded as if she didn't have a care in the world other than tonight's supper. "Isaac, this is David Riehl. He lives here in Evergreen Corners, and he's been helping, too."

The two men shook hands, sizing each other up. She wasn't sure what they were looking for as they appraised each other.

"So you're one of the volunteers?" Isaac asked.

"I'm working with Abby on a program for the teen volunteers."

Her brother turned to her. "You are?"

"Glen asked us last week to put together a program," she said quietly. "Glen wants to make sure the teenagers understand they can move closer to God at the same time they're offering their help."

Isaac nodded. "Hmm…that's a *gut* idea."

"I thought so," she said.

"*We* thought so," David said.

Why had he used a tone that challenged her older brother? Isaac, in spite of his officious exterior, was eager to get the residents of Evergreen Corners into their homes again.

"Your idea, Abby?" Isaac asked.

"No. It was Glen's." She turned toward the community center. "Excuse me. I need to get to work."

Her hope that would end the discussion failed when Isaac said, "I'm curious why Glen asked you two to work on the program."

"My daughter is one of the teens," David replied. "And the kids are fond of Abby. It may have to do with the cookies she has waiting for them every day after school."

"So that's how you two met?"

Abby shot her brother a frown. Hadn't they just agreed to no matchmaking? Not that Isaac would consider *Englisch* David a proper match for her.

"We met," she explained, "when David came to fix the freezer at the community center." She laughed, hoping it sounded natural. "As I heard someone once say, not all superheroes wear capes."

Isaac gave her a puzzled frown but she wagged a finger at him. "Don't pretend with me, Isaac Kauffman. I know you used to read comic books and I've heard you say those very words."

"You know about the comic books?"

"If you'd wanted to keep them a secret, you should have found a better place to hide them than in the hayloft, where you kept your radio. I found your stash when I was looking for somewhere to put the bottle of fingernail polish one of the neighbor girls gave me."

"Which one?"

Again she laughed and this time it was an honest one. "Do you think I'm going to tell you? I wouldn't want to get a respectable Amish *mamm* in trouble." She looked at David and smiled. "We've all done things better left in the past, ain't so?"

"If you think I'm going to answer that loaded question, think again. I'm not sure what the statute of limitations is on my teen mistakes."

She wanted to hug him for following her lead in leaving the heavier topics behind. When Isaac announced he'd lingered too long and had to get to the school to meet with Glen, she kept her sigh of relief silent. She and her brother needed to have a talk straightaway before he made things worse with his mistaken assumptions. She glanced at David's taut face as he watched her brother walk away and hoped it wasn't already too late.

David pushed down his irritation. His fingers curled into fists at his sides. Until he'd met Isaac Kauffman, he'd been wondering if his parents had been mistaken in their negative opinions of the Amish. The plain people he'd met in Evergreen Corners were generous, caring folks eager to walk in the path they believed God had for them. He'd worked several times with Michael Miller, a plain man who'd come to Evergreen Corners to help and then decided to stay to make the village his home. Michael oversaw one of the building sites and he'd asked David to come check some of the mechanicals before they were hooked up in the new houses.

Michael was a good man, hardworking, honest and with a wry sense of humor. David enjoyed chatting with him, often about their kids. Michael's were young, but the challenges of being a father were the same whether a man was Amish or *Englisch*.

Isaac fit the description his parents had given him of the stiff-necked men and women who'd driven them away. David could imagine Isaac banishing those who disagreed with him.

Stop it! Isaac was Abby's brother, a brother she respected and cared about. David had been wrong in his first impressions of people before and he couldn't make that error again.

As if she could sense his uneasy thoughts, she said, "You and Mikayla should come for supper tonight so you can get to know Isaac better."

"At the community center?"

She smiled. "In spite of how it must seem to everyone, I don't spend every hour of every day there. Today, I'm working on preparations for the evening meal, but not the meal itself."

"So you want to cook for us on your evening off?"

"I'll be cooking for Isaac and myself." Her eyes twinkled like sunshine through a pine forest. "And I've gotten so used to cooking for a crowd I don't think he'll be able to eat it all."

Was she trying to avoid being alone with her overbearing brother?

Whether that was the reason or not, he heard himself accepting the invitation. Mikayla would be thrilled, though he had to wonder what she'd make of Abby's brother.

Abby's smile sent unexpected sensation zinging through him like lightning. Her cheery wave as she rushed along the green made him grin. No matter how much he'd tried to ignore it, her charming warmth was winning him over as it had Mikayla.

To count Abby as a friend would go against everything his parents had taught him. He thought of giving them a call and talking about how she was different from the Amish they'd described. He didn't want to bring up old injuries and open them anew.

The cold splash of reality reminded him that he needed to get to the school cafeteria to fix the dishwasher that refused to pump water out. He would concentrate on his task and try to forget about her sparkling green eyes.

And David almost succeeded, though wisps of Abby's smile kept invading his mind as he worked on the dishwasher. Two hours later, he was finished and the cafeteria workers were filling the dishwasher so they could complete their work and head home to their families. He nodded to the thanks they called out to him.

He walked into the corridor, which was almost silent with school dismissed for the day. He heard bits of conversation from a room across the hall and saw several teachers and students gathered around a table.

Hurrying along, he glanced at his watch.

He had just enough time to go home and get cleaned up before he collected Mikayla at the community center. He'd made an effort each day to stop by so she didn't have to walk home alone. Neither of them spoke of the bullies, but he guessed he wasn't the only parent keeping a close eye on the teens. Not once had Mikayla complained about him picking her up, which he took as a sign she was worried about being the next victim.

"Do you have a moment, David?"

His eyes widened when he saw Isaac Kauffman striding toward him.

"Certainly," he replied. "Can I help you with something?"

"*Ja.*" Isaac stopped in front of him. He glanced at an open door leading into a classroom. "We can talk in there. I wish you to know my opinion on an important matter."

Again, David was amazed a vivacious woman like Abby Kauffman could be related to the far too serious Isaac. She seemed to care about everyone, and her brother acted as if he'd be fine if everyone followed his orders.

Memories of his parents talking about the unbending Amish flooded his mind. His mother and father had used the words *the deacon* and *the ordained men* as if they spoke of the worst kind of people. Though they'd never shared any specifics about what the Amish leaders had done, he hadn't been able to mistake their contempt for the men who refused to listen to anyone's opinions but their own.

Now Isaac wanted to air *his* opinions.

Quelling his uneasy thoughts, David walked into the room after Abby's brother. He leaned against the wall and faced the man who was taller than his own six feet.

The other man crossed to look out the window at the playground. For a long moment he stared out the window; then he faced David.

"After my meeting with Glen, I went to the community center. Abby told me more about the program to put an end to the bullying that's been going on. I'm not surprised she jumped in to help." His austere face creased in a smile that came and went swiftly. "And she mentioned you have a teenage daughter, so I guess I can understand why you want to be involved."

"That sums it up." He wasn't going to explain to a stranger his complicated feelings about working with Abby. If he spoke of his discomfort at spending so much time with an Amish woman, he'd insult her brother. If he broached the topic of how he was at his wits' end in his efforts to convince Mikayla to open up to him, he was sure to embarrass himself.

"You are *Englisch*, David, so you may not understand it isn't the Amish way to become engulfed in the problems of nonplain folks."

"I do understand." *And you plain people won't consider the needs of those who count themselves as one of you.*

He was glad he'd halted that from bursting past his lips. It was a petty thought when the plain folks had come to Evergreen Corners to help and never asked for anything in return.

"That's why I think it would be for the best if Abby didn't continue working with *Englisch* teens." Isaac turned back to the window.

"You expect her to stop helping?" A guffaw burst from him. "Abby Kauffman stop helping people? Is that even possible?"

"It needs to be."

David pushed aside his amusement when he saw Isaac had taken his laugh the wrong way. It hadn't been his intention to insult Abby's stuffy brother.

"I think you're fighting an impossible battle," David said. "What do you expect me to say to her when she asks me about plans for the kids?"

Isaac tensed. "I don't expect you to speak to her about this. I wanted to let you know why she won't be working with you any longer."

"You believe she'll stop working with the teens because you tell her to?"

"I am her older brother."

When Isaac didn't add more, David realized the man thought that answer was explanation enough. "Abby may not be willing to accept your authority on this."

"Why wouldn't she?" For the first time since he'd turned away, Isaac looked at him.

David shrugged. "You tell me. She's *your* sister, so you know her better than I do. Since I first met her, I've learned one thing about Abby Kauffman. I don't know how she was before she came here, but she has made her job here the center of her life. I don't think you'll be able to talk her out of that."

For the first time Isaac loosened up enough to sigh with obvious frustration. "You're not telling me anything I don't know, but she can't think only of helping people here. Nor can I. Abby is my sister, and I need to watch over her." He cared about his sister. "My sister needs to think of her future, as well."

"I can't argue with that." How he longed to tell Abby's brother to stop worrying! Abby's future wasn't with the son of runaway Amish.

Even as he thought of her spending time with some other man, another twinge raced through him. Only this one left a searing pain in its wake as it hit his heart.

Chapter Six

Clattering pans together was a *gut* way to work off frustration, Abby decided as she searched for the exact cookie tray she wanted to put beneath the cherry pies she had ready to go into the second oven. The other was filled with pans of chocolate-chip cookies.

Isaac had refused to tell her where he'd gone this afternoon, and she'd discovered why half an hour ago. She'd happened to overhear a couple of the *Englisch* volunteers talking about whether David would be joining their teams at the new houses. They'd overheard her brother talking with David. That, the *Englischers* were certain, was a sign David would be bringing his skills more often to the new house sites.

She wasn't so sure.

Isaac had rushed out after he'd learned more about the job Glen had given her and David.

Knowing her brother as she did, she should have guessed he'd gone to see David so he could remind David an Amish woman shouldn't marry an *Englischer*. She wanted to remind her brother she was a grown woman, but that wouldn't make any difference. Isaac saw it as his job to watch over his only sister until the day she exchanged vows with an Amish man of whom he approved. For Isaac, her future was an unfinished detail, and he hated leaving anything undone.

What could she say to him? *Don't care about me as much as you do?* She appreciated how much he worried about her. To be honest, in spite of teasing him about leaving their younger brother in charge of the farm, she was always shocked when he left long enough to come and help in Evergreen Corners. He was torn between his duty to family and his duty to help others as Jesus urged His disciples to do.

It is more blessed to give than to receive. That was one of the earliest lessons the *kinder* in her family had learned. She and Isaac had taken that verse from Acts to heart.

"Hey, Abby!"

Her grumpy mood vanished at Mikayla's voice. The girl sounded carefree, a *gut* sign she hadn't had a run-in with the bullies after school.

In fact, the bullies hadn't bothered anyone the last few days. It might have been only a reprieve, but Abby prayed they'd given up their hurtful ways and found better venues to expend their energy.

"Hey yourself, Mikayla." Abby bent to take the pans of cookies out of the oven and slid them, one at a time, onto the butcher-block counter next to the stove. With the ease of practice, she used a spatula to lift the cookies from the trays to the aluminum foil where they could cool. "The other kids have stopped by already and headed out to where they're working today. Aren't you joining them?"

"I am, but I came to talk to you first. Do you know Doris Blomgren?" Mikayla came into the kitchen and reached around Abby to snag a chocolate-chip cookie.

"Be careful! Those are hot."

Bouncing the cookie from hand to hand, the girl grimaced. "You could have warned me."

"I would have told you to be careful if I'd known you were going to grab one right after you watched me take them out of the oven. Would that have stopped you?"

"Probably not. Your cookies are the best, Abby." After taking a bite of the soft cookie and melted chocolate, she sighed. "So good." She didn't pause before she asked again. "Do you know Doris Blomgren?"

"*Ja*. I should say I know of her, because we've

never met. She's been generous in sending casseroles over to share with the volunteers."

"She's Jack's aunt." Her nose wrinkled. "Maybe his great-aunt. Anyhow, she's a nice old lady."

Abby had to wonder how old "old" was in Mikayla's estimation. It could mean Doris was any age from forty up. Maybe even in her thirties. To a teenager, that was *old*.

"She needs help with something," Mikayla said, "and I thought we might be able to help."

"We? You and me?" Abby asked as she set the cookie sheets aside to reuse with the next batch to put into the oven.

"No, the teen volunteers. I heard David talking on the phone to Glen about the project you two are supposed to be working on with us."

Delighted the girl was interested in a project that would mean spending more time with her guardian, Abby said, "We're hoping to do projects and fun events."

"Fun? David?"

The girl's words echoed what David had said at the diner. Was he averse to having a *gut* time? No, he'd said someone else had told him he wasn't fun.

Abby asked, "Do you think he's fun?"

The girl looked away, lowering her eyes. The motion told Abby everything she needed to confirm her suspicions. *Daed* and daughter were leading parallel lives, residing under the same roof but having little interaction. Sorrow bubbled tears into her eyes because she couldn't imagine anything sadder than two people resisting anything that would make them a family.

"Well," Abby said, trying to sound casual, "if you don't think he's fun, maybe you think he's funny, too."

"Too?" The teenager stared in astonishment. "You think David is funny?"

"He's always saying things that make me laugh. He's got a way with words, I guess you could say."

"Really?"

"It's subtle, ain't so?" She reached for the bottle so she could pour a thin sheen of oil on the cookie sheets. "I find I've got to listen for the jokes he's making. If I wasn't paying attention, they'd probably go right over my head."

She held her breath, watching as the girl digested her words. It was a long shot, Abby knew, but if Mikayla listened more to what David had to say, there was a chance they could become closer.

When Mikayla mumbled a noncommittal answer, Abby let her breath sift through her teeth. Getting the two to see their lives would be enriched by each other was going to be more difficult than she'd thought.

She spooned dough onto the cookie sheet. Once she finished baking this batch, she would head to the apartment and prepare supper for herself, Isaac and their guests. Maybe she'd have another opportunity then to persuade Mikayla to spend more time with her guardian.

"Abby, what do you say we make our first project helping Doris Blomgren?"

Putting the trays into the oven and setting the timer, Abby asked, "What does Doris need?"

Mikayla snatched another cookie and, as she ate it, explained how she'd known Doris most of her life. "She was my grandmother's best friend. She has an old-fashioned sewing machine that isn't working. Maybe we can help her get it fixed."

"All of us? Fixing an old sewing machine sounds like something David can do on his own."

"It is."

"But?" she asked when the girl again wouldn't meet her eyes.

"Mrs. Blomgren is pretty old-fashioned as well as old." Mikayla rolled her eyes. "She must be close to a hundred."

"Really?"

Lifting her phone, Mikayla tapped it a couple

of times and handed it to Abby. "That's Mrs. Blomgren in the photo. See? She's ancient!"

The picture was blurred, but, squinting, Abby could make out the image of a woman. She had pure white hair, and her hands, resting on the arms of an overstuffed chair, were wrinkled. Perhaps her face was as well, but Abby couldn't tell by the photo.

A man stood next to the chair where the woman sat. Like Doris, the man's face wasn't clear. Could that be Mikayla's *daed*? Was that why she kept such an out-of-focus photo?

Handing the phone to Mikayla, she said, "She looks to be in her seventies or eighties."

"Maybe, but she acts like she was born and raised in Victorian times. She says she doesn't think David should be alone with her in her house for the time it'll take to fix the sewing machine."

"Then why doesn't he take it to his shop to fix it?"

"A good question" came the answer in a deeper voice.

She looked over her shoulder to see David crossing the community center's main room. His coat was unzipped and his bright yellow-and-green winter hat and dark gloves were nowhere to be seen.

Had it warmed up outside? It suddenly felt

much hotter inside the kitchen. As if both ovens were set on Broil and each of the dozen burners lit. She realized the warmth came from within her as he entered the kitchen. She was startled by how pleased she was to see him.

She was the only one. Mikayla said something under her breath, grabbed her coat and rushed out of the kitchen.

"Mikayla!" Abby called after her. "Don't you want to tell David about your great idea?"

"You tell him! I've got to go—I should be—" The outer door slammed behind her.

Abby looked at David. He held up a hand before she could speak.

"Don't apologize, Abby," he said in a clipped tone. "You didn't do anything to make her run off."

"Nor did you."

"And that's the problem." He sighed. "How can you fix something when you don't have any idea what's wrong?"

Abby wished she had an answer for him but, for once, she couldn't see a quick solution to a problem and how she might have been able to help resolve it.

David saw the sorrow on Abby's expressive face and he wanted to kick himself...again. First, his arrival had sent his daughter fleeing. Now he'd upset Abby. Though he didn't want to admit it, maybe her brother was right to worry about David spending so much time with her. Everything he did seemed to distress those around him.

Stop it! he told himself as he had so many times before. He'd made the cafeteria workers happy by fixing the dishwasher. Too bad relationships didn't come with user manuals and a way to repair them with a simple hand tool.

If it'd been easy to mend problems among people, his parents would have discovered how long ago. They would have put to rest the bad memories of their lives among the Amish. Though they'd pretended they had, they hadn't, because anytime he tried to initiate a discussion about his past, they shut him down.

Pushing those thoughts aside, because each day he spent with Abby made him more baffled about his parents' opinions, he asked, "What great idea has Mikayla had?"

He listened while Abby took cookies out of the oven and outlined what his daughter had told her. Not sure why Mikayla wouldn't have wanted to share with him, he said, "I'd be glad to fix Doris's sewing machine for her. I don't know how we would involve the teens."

"I said the same thing. According to Mikayla, Doris Blomgren believes she needs a chaperone so her neighbors won't gossip about a man being behind her closed doors while her sewing machine is repaired."

When her lips twitched, he felt his do the same. He hadn't thought he'd be able to smile after his conversation with her brother. "I'm not surprised, because Doris has her own view of the world and nobody's going to change her mind at this late date."

"What do you think of it being a project for the teenagers?"

"It would give us the answer to the riddle of how many people it takes to fix a treadle sewing machine."

He heard a soft sound behind him. Shock riveted him when he realized it was Mikayla muffling a laugh. Mikayla? She'd come back? Though he wanted to turn and see for himself that she'd found his weak joke funny, he didn't. Would she stop laughing if she realized he'd heard her?

When Abby looked past him, he rested one elbow on the counter with what he hoped looked like nonchalance. He didn't say anything as Mikayla explained she couldn't show up without cookies. Abby wrapped up almost two dozen of the delicious smelling cookies and handed them to Mikayla.

"Anything else?" Abby asked.

"Not now," his daughter said before rushing for the door.

"Don't be too late. We're having supper at Abby's tonight," David called.

He thought she wasn't going to respond, but she paused and faced them. "Are we really having supper tonight with you, Abby?"

"*Ja*, with me and my brother."

"Okay." Mikayla glared at him before leaving.

He sighed, wondering if he'd ever figure out his daughter.

"At least, she likes the idea of joining us for supper." Abby gave him a sympathetic smile as she put the cookie sheet into the sink to soak. He was no longer amazed she seemed privy to his thoughts, even when they were a jumble in his head. "Our apartment is neutral territory. Maybe she'll open up to you a bit more while you're there."

"I hope so." He did because he was running out of ideas on how to reach the girl.

Chapter Seven

When she heard the knock on the apartment door, Abby emerged from the tiny kitchen into the not much bigger living room. She smiled when her brother opened the door to reveal David and Mikayla on the other side.

"*Komm* in!" she called. "You're right on time."

Her cheery tone seemed to fall on deaf ears because Isaac scowled as he let their guests in. David sidled past her brother, acting as if he anticipated an attack at any moment. Mikayla hurried across the small living room to stand beside Abby, apparently hoping to be out of the way of any angry words.

For a moment, Abby was tempted to tell Mikayla not to worry. Isaac had assured her less than five minutes ago he'd say nothing to David about her participation in the youth group. As she watched the two men eye each other, she wondered if she should have asked her brother to act as if the conversation at the school had never happened.

Isaac saw the whole world in black and white. Trying to convince him to be any other way would have been futile.

"Supper is ready," she said to break the silence. "Mikayla, why don't you and David take off your coats and leave them on the sofa? Then you can join us in the kitchen." She hooked a thumb over her shoulder. "Right through this door." Without pausing, she said, "Isaac, I could use your help in getting the roast on the table."

Her brother looked at her, startled. An Amish kitchen was a woman's domain and a male entered it only to eat.

"I was going to get the extra chairs…" he began.

"That can wait. Lots to do before we're ready to sit down, and I could use your help." She *did* need his cooperation to make the evening pleasant.

She let a soft sigh drift past her lips as her brother went into the kitchen. Isaac was going to try his best to make their guests feel welcome. Again, she should have expected that. Being hospitable—even to outsiders—was an essential tenet of the plain people.

Mikayla asked question after question about

the process of making gravy, and Abby answered each one. She guessed Mikayla was wary of letting silence fall again.

Abby was, too, which was why she kept up a steady monologue. "Mikayla, will you get the butter out of the fridge? It's on the top shelf of the door. The bread was made today. Not by me. I picked it up at the diner. You know they have a nice selection of breads there. Do you know what chowchow is, Mikayla? It's in the clear bowl with the dark blue top, on the second shelf in the fridge. Will you put it on the table, too? I'll get the mashed potatoes into another bowl and then I'll pour out the gravy, and we'll be set to go. We…"

Her voice trailed away when she saw regret in David's eyes. His gaze was on his daughter. He looked at Abby and quickly away. Sadness sifted through her. David and Mikayla led overlapping lives but had raised barriers between them. She prayed they'd find a way to break through.

"Where do you want the roast, Abby?" asked Isaac, drawing her attention to him.

She flinched, knowing he'd been aware of that fleeting moment when her eyes and David's had connected.

"On the table anywhere," she answered, the raw heat of tears filling her throat.

Had this been the worst idea she'd had since the night of the buggy race accident? It was unlikely anyone would be injured tonight, but the tension in the room was strangling her.

When Isaac went to get extra chairs from the garage downstairs, David moved closer to the stove.

"Maybe we should go," he said. "Your brother is unhappy about us being here."

"No," she said, not giving herself the opportunity to admit he was right. "We invited you for supper, and I doubt you've got much of anything in the house to make a meal for yourself and Mikayla."

"We can order pizza."

She looked into the living room, where the girl perched on the well-broken-in sofa, paging through the latest copy of the *Budget*. Abby doubted the teenager was pausing to read news from plain communities published in the letters the newspaper's correspondents had submitted from around the world. The girl was hunched into herself.

"Did something happen to her?" Abby asked, not wanting to alert the girl that they were talking about her.

David's mouth hardened. "Those bullies went after Mikayla and Lily DeMent today on their way home from the site where they've been volunteering."

She gasped. "Are they okay?"

"So far the bullies are using just words."

"Words hurt."

His expression eased. "That sounds like the voice of experience."

"I've seen this happen to others." *And to myself,* she added silently.

"I wish I knew how to halt this. I keep a close eye on her and the other kids, but somehow the bullies find out when I'm not around. Same with the other kids' parents."

"I'll keep praying that a solution will be found."

"Thank you, Abby." He put a hand on her shoulder. "I appreciate that more than I can say. I—"

David pulled back from her as the outer door opened and Isaac walked in. She realized how close they'd been standing. If her brother had seen, nothing she said would persuade him that she and David both understood they could be no more than friends.

Abby ignored her anxiety when Isaac set the chairs by the table. Mikayla came in to join them. When Abby motioned for them to take their seats, she was glad to see David and his daughter sitting side by side. The other side of

the table was left for her and Isaac. Her brother
hesitated for a long moment, and she knew he
was trying to decide what was worse: him sitting across from David or her. When he pulled
out the chair opposite Mikayla, she wished she
could reassure her brother that he had nothing
to worry about.

She couldn't. Not when her heart jumped
for joy at something as silly as being able to
face David throughout the meal. Silencing that
thought, she set the mashed potatoes and a big
bowl of dark gravy on the small table before she
pulled out her own chair.

"We pray silently," Isaac said after she sat,
"but you're welcome to say grace aloud if you
wish."

Mikayla leaned forward. "What do you
pray?"

"My gratitude for the food on our table and
those around it," Isaac said in his most pomp-
ous tone.

When the girl quelled, Abby jumped in to say,
"*Ja*, but when I was a little girl I used to say the
Lord's Prayer as many times as fast as I could
before *Daed* gave us the signal to begin eating."

She was amazed when Isaac asked, "You did
that?" She didn't want him to scold her in front
of their company. Then he grinned. "I did the
same thing. I got up to four repetitions com-

pleted one time when *Grossdawdi* Kauffman was at the table."

Laughing, she looked across the table at David and Mikayla. "When we were young, we loved our *grossdawdi*. Our grandfather. However, he took the longest time to say grace. If one of us became antsy because we were hungry, he'd take longer because he thought we should be focused on gratitude, not the delicious food *Grossmammi* put on the table." She winked at her brother. "Four, huh? That's got to be a record."

"Haven't heard of anyone who's ever done more." He puffed his chest out in a false pose of pride. That brought laughter from them.

As they bent their heads for grace, the first thing Abby thanked God for was how the conversation had turned so that the glowers and silences had become *gut* humor. The distrust Isaac had for David wasn't gone, but she hoped, for the next few hours, it could be forgotten.

Abby rose before the sun the next morning to have *kaffi* brewing while she cooked breakfast for Isaac. Though he didn't have to milk while he was in the village, he kept the same hours he did up north.

Isaac said nothing more than a mumbled *gute mariye* as he sat at the table now edged again only by two chairs. He'd waited until she'd put their eggs, bacon and toast on the table along with the pot of *kaffi* and had pulled out her own chair. Bending his head for grace, he remained silent. That silence she understood.

As she did almost every time she prayed, she began by thanking the *gut* Lord for His kindness in bringing her to Evergreen Corners, where she could do His work. She'd asked for healing for her battered heart and He had led her to a place where she was kept so busy she seldom had time to think about the past and the mistakes she'd made.

Isaac cleared his throat, raised his head and reached for his fork. Before he took a single bite, he said, "After hearing you and David Riehl talk about your plans for the youth group last night, it's clear to me you're spending too much time with this *Englischer*."

Her relief at how well the previous night had gone sifted away. "I spend lots of time with lots of *Englischers*. There aren't many plain folk in Evergreen Corners. Even the Mennonites here aren't conservative. They drive cars and have TVs and computers." She knew she was avoiding the conversation about David that she didn't want to have, but she also was aware of the fact her brother wouldn't be put off any longer from saying what was on his mind.

"Abby, you should be more serious."

"I'm serious about helping people get back into their homes and businesses." She picked up a piece of toast and buttered it, though her appetite had vanished. "As you are, Isaac."

"You need to think of your future. You don't want to become an *alt maedel*."

She wasn't bothered by his concerns about her never marrying and being labeled an old maid, but she wouldn't say that to Isaac. If she did, he'd try to find another way to convince her to heed his worries about her future if she didn't wed.

"Of course, I don't," she replied, putting the toast next to the rest of her untouched breakfast, "but for now, I've committed to helping here."

"Someone else can step in to do your job. You must never forget how important it is not to create gossip about yourself."

"Wouldn't I create more gossip if I walked away from what I'd promised to do?" Getting up to put the *kaffi* pot on the stove, she kept him from seeing her grimace.

She could imagine how he'd react if she said the same thing to him. Though with her brother's skills as a mason and being able to lay out a foundation with square corners, he might not be as easy to replace as a cook.

"Isaac, you asked me to come with you and our cousins to Evergreen Corners."

"I did, but I didn't think you would want to stay for months and months. I'm beginning to wonder if you ever intend to come home."

She faced him and saw disconcertment lining his forehead. If she'd needed proof he cared about her, there it was. However, she couldn't let his sense of obligation for her future persuade her into doing something that would ruin the rest of her life.

"Of course, I intend to come back to our farm." She let her own devotion to her family fill her voice. "My home is with you and the rest of our family, but right now, helping here is where I can best serve God and His people. He has led me to guiding a group of teenagers closer to Him. How can I walk away from that?"

"You're changing the subject again."

"I thought what I'm going to do in the future was the subject." She came to the table and sat beside him.

"David Riehl is the subject. I don't like how much time you're already spending with him. You should be enjoying the company of young men who might be willing to marry you."

This time Abby couldn't hide her frown. "*Willing* to marry me? Do you think I'm such an *alt maedel* that someone has to settle for me?"

"No, no." Issac had the decency to appear embarrassed and she hoped he'd realized he shouldn't be harping on the subject. He hadn't announced any plans to wed, either. "But, Abby, it's an older brother's place to look after his younger sister."

"If you're worried about anything between David and me, stop. David is an *Englischer*. I'm plain. We can be friends but nothing more. We're working together to help the teens learn to trust God will guide them to know how to deal with these bullies." She was glad he couldn't hear her thoughts because a pinch of sadness warned her that, in spite of her words, she'd thought about sharing more with David than friendship. No! She was trying to help him build a better relationship with his daughter, not with her! Annoyance at her own thoughts sharpened her tone. "You know I know that, Isaac. Why are you acting so anxious over this?"

"Because I know your heart hasn't given you the best advice before."

She froze, horrified that Isaac would throw the past at her now in an effort to prove his point. Didn't he realize that every day, every decision she made was colored by what had happened the night Bert Fetter was almost killed during the buggy race?

"Es dutt mir leed," he said, breaking the silence.

"I know you're sorry."

"I didn't say that to hurt you, only to…" He sighed. "I want to make sure you don't get hurt again, little sister."

She continued to stare at her plate and her untouched breakfast. The eggs had congealed. No matter, because she doubted she could eat a single bite anyhow. "I understand that, but I also know how hard I work so I won't make the same mistake twice. I've learned my lesson, and listening to my heart is the last thing I'm ever going to do again."

Had that been a knock at the barn door?

David switched off the battery-operated screwdriver he'd been using to open the underside of a toaster. Looking over his shoulder, he saw a silhouette in the doorway of the old barn he'd turned into a repair shop.

Sunlight streamed through the translucent shape of a heart-shaped *kapp* atop a head that was the right height to belong to Abby Kauffman. Of course, it was Abby. Why would any other plain woman be standing by his shop door?

Why was *Abby* there?

He grimaced. What had her brother said to her after he and Mikayla had left? David doubted Isaac had been as uncommunicative as

Mikayla after supper last night. Every attempt he'd made to get his daughter to talk about the incident with Hunter Keyes and the other bullies had been fruitless. She was upset, but she didn't want to tell him what had occurred.

Had Mikayla spoken to Abby about it? Was that why Abby was knocking on his door now?

"David, are you inside?" she called as she rapped her knuckles against the door again.

Knowing he was lost in the shadows because the barn's few windows were draped with dusty spiderwebs, he brushed crumbs from the toaster off his hands. He opened the door and drew in a deep breath when he saw how the spring sunshine shone off her golden hair. She looked the embodiment of spring with her crisp white *kapp* and pale pink dress that was the color of the hearts of the apple blossoms that soon would burst open.

"Come on in," he said once he got both his breath and voice back, though he wanted to ask if she'd talked to Mikayla about the bullies. "How are you today?"

"I'm fine. I wanted to let you know that I spoke with Doris Blomgren. She's agreed for the two of us to come to her house the day after tomorrow. I've got time after lunch. Would that work for you?"

"Let me check." He ignored his disappointment that Abby hadn't come to talk to him about his daughter. He went to a simple plank stretched across two sawhorses. Opening a calendar on top of it, he flipped the page to the new week. "Michael Miller asked me to stop by his building site that afternoon to look at a circular saw that isn't working. It shouldn't take long. How does two work for you?"

"I need to be at the community center by three at the latest."

"We're just looking at her sewing machine, so it won't take long."

"Sounds *gut*." She smiled, and his center melted.

Why did the first woman who'd made him react like that in years have to be Amish? She'd never given him any suggestion she was open to any relationship other than friendship. It was good that at least one of them had their head screwed on right.

To cover up his hesitation, he asked with what he hoped sounded like irony, "Do you think I can make hundred-plus-year-old parts appear when I snap my fingers?"

Abby smiled, and he was delighted to see a dimple on either side of her mouth. How had he missed those before now?

"I've heard you're the best in town," she replied in the same teasing tone, "at repairing anything. Maybe you can make parts appear as you need them."

He laughed and was surprised when his shoulders eased from the taut line they'd assumed the night he'd heard of Boyd's death. They'd grown more rigid when he'd discovered Boyd's house had been washed away by the flood. Had they been so stiff for almost a year?

"I'll do my best," he said, "but I'm not that good."

"I don't think you'll need to. Doris may be stubborn and more than a bit old-fashioned, but she seems kind."

When she started to turn to leave, he heard himself asking, "Would you like a tour of the shop?"

Had he lost the last vestiges of his mind? He should be relieved she wasn't planning to linger. She hadn't flirted or led him on. She was being the friend she wished him to be. He knew she was smart, but, for a moment, he wanted to be foolish.

He almost laughed again. Foolish? His ex would have snorted in derision if he'd described himself that way. Chelsea's favorite words for him had been *dull* and *boring* and *stick-in-the-mud*. And maybe he had been when he was with her, because, in retrospect, he'd come to realize they'd had too little in common. She'd wanted to go barhopping, and he'd liked to spend a quiet evening with a close friends.

"*Danki*, David," Abby said, bringing his attention back to her. "But what I'd really like is a tour of your big barn."

"The big barn?"

"*Ja*. Barns here in Vermont are different from the ones I'm familiar with in Lancaster County."

"I thought you lived in the Northeast Kingdom."

She smiled again when he used the common term for the section of the state that bordered both New Hampshire and Canada. "Our dairy barn is a bank barn like the one we had in Lancaster County. Your barn isn't built into a hillside like those."

"All right. C'mon." He opened the door. The fresh breeze refused to surrender its chill and he zipped his light brown barn coat and closed the snaps along the front.

Walking beside him, Abby wrapped her arms around herself as if she could hold off the cold. Her black coat was made of thick wool, and she wore thick socks beneath her dress that peeked from beneath the hem of her coat. Her bonnet protected her from the wind, but he guessed it became a wind tunnel when they turned into the breeze.

"Whew," she murmured once inside after he'd

opened the small door next to the huge sliding one on the front of the barn.

Dust motes danced in a crazy swirl as the wind found every crevice in the barn's walls and around the windows. A miniature tornado twirled, raising remnants of hay and chaff off the concrete floor. Overhead came the sound of swallows disturbed by the eddies of air reaching into their haven in the hayloft.

Abby scanned the space. He watched as she turned around, taking in everything. When she took a deep breath, he did the same. It was flavored with the aromas of a barn, the dry odor of the hay as well as the lush scents of oats and other grains.

"You don't keep any animals in here?" she asked. "I don't smell them."

"I used to have a few chickens, two horses, a donkey and an ornery old goat when I was a kid. When my repair business started to consume my time, it wasn't fair to animals not to be fed and cared for on a regular schedule."

"True." She faced him. "So you grew up on this farm?"

"From the time I began school. My parents sold it to me when they decided they wanted to live somewhere else."

"It's interesting to see how much is the same about this barn and the ones I'm familiar with."

She walked to a ladder that was made of thick pegs set into two uprights supporting the roof. Touching them, she said, "I've seen something that looks like this in almost every barn I've been in. Is this ladder the only way to reach the hayloft?"

"No, but the hay had to be pulled up to the hayloft." He gestured for her to follow him over to a nearby window. Wiping the dust off the panes with the elbow of his coat, he pointed upward. "See that small extension sticking out from gable end? It's above a door on the upper floor. It's called a hay hood. A pulley was attached there to lift the hay up to the loft. That door is nailed shut now because I didn't want any kids trying to sneak in. Plenty of the boards in the loft floor are rotted. One of these days, in my spare time, I'll look into replacing them."

"What would you use the space for?" She edged back from the window and looked up again.

"Apartments are always at a premium around here, especially ones for families with lower incomes. There's enough room upstairs for a couple of two-bedroom apartments. I'd add extra windows so the renters could enjoy views of the mountains." He gave her a crooked smile. "Sometimes I think I should talk Mikayla into helping me, so we could work on the project together. But first, I'd have to convince her to say more than two words in a row to me."

"She will."

"I wish I could be as sure of that. The few times I've gotten her to talk to me, she says no to anything I suggest. I know she's grieving, but I don't want heartache to be her life."

"It won't be, David." She wiped dust off the sleeve of his coat. It was a motion he could imagine her doing with the teens, but he was riveted by the craving to pull her closer. He longed to know how she would feel in his arms, how her soft mouth would taste, the sweet scent of her hair.

He was saved from his own thoughts when she said, "Give Mikayla time, David. Each of us mourns differently."

"I wish she'd be more positive about the things I suggest."

"She's a teenager. Give her the benefit of the doubt and stay optimistic that things will work out. She's grateful to you, though she seldom shows it."

Mikayla was grateful? That was news to him, especially after last night when the only thing she'd said had been a grudging good-night before she'd gone upstairs to her room the minute they'd returned home.

He wanted to believe Abby, but everything

in his world had turned upside down in the past year. First, he'd become the father of a teenager. Now he'd met a woman who made him question everything his parents had ever told him about the Amish.

After he walked out of the barn with Abby, he told her he'd see her in a couple of days at the Blomgren house. She gave him a quick wave and hurried down the drive between his house and the shop. He wished there was a reason to ask her to stay longer. It didn't have to be a good reason.

But not the truth that he couldn't stop thinking about: how much he wanted to kiss her.

Chapter Eight

"There. That should do it." David straightened and wiped his hands on his trousers. "Remind your workers to clean out the sawdust from around the blade at the end of every day, so it doesn't start building up."

With a chuckle, Michael Miller settled his black wool hat on his head. "I do remind them. They tell me they forget." He shook his head. "I'll keep after them. We can't work if our tools don't."

Closing his toolbox, David said, "I'm amazed you use power tools. I thought electricity was off-limits to you Amish."

"No, it's not off-limits. We *choose* not to connect our homes to the power grid but we use what we have to in order to get a job done."

"I don't understand why one's okay and the other isn't."

His friend leaned against an idle skid steer. Crossing his arms in front of him, he smiled. "That confuses a lot of folks, but it's simple. We want the focus in our homes to be on God and our families. Not television shows or the internet or whatever else is going on. The choices our ancestors made were intended to keep us more involved with each other and less caught up in the concerns of the rest of the world."

He thought of how Mikayla spent each evening in her room, plugged into social media and distancing herself from him. Would it be different if they lived a plain life?

The thought startled him. As he listened to Michael explain the Amish used buggies because it also allowed them more time with family and close neighbors, he wondered if that was the reason his parents had left. They'd often traveled during their careers with the successful construction company his father had built from the ground up, leaving David with sitters when he was too young to be by himself. He'd assumed family was important to them, but he now began to wonder.

As he drove to Doris Blomgren's house later, David couldn't shake the questions from his head. Why *had* his parents abandoned everything they'd known to strike out on their own?

David had no answers and more questions

to taunt him as he got out of his well-used red truck in front of Doris's house. He wasn't surprised to see Abby waiting by the front walk. He hoped she hadn't been there long. Checking out the circular saw had taken longer than he'd planned.

"Sorry I'm late," he said.

"You're right on time," she replied when he reached the sidewalk.

He glanced at his watch and saw that she was right. "The clock in the truck must be running fast." He chuckled. "The only thing about that old piece of junk that is."

"Shall we go inside? I've seen Doris peeking out the windows several times, so I know she's eager to talk to us."

"Lead the way."

He followed her along the sidewalk and up the steps to the small front porch. There was nothing otherwise modest about the old house. Wings wandered in every possible direction and he wondered when each had been added to the original building. Three stories high, it was topped by a widow's walk enclosed in glass.

Abby rang the bell and the door opened. Doris Blomgren was a bright sprite of a woman. Her pure white hair was braided and arranged in a coronet on her head. She wore a light pink shirtwaist dress with a garish print that belonged to a time more than sixty years ago. A Donna Reed type with a pearl necklace to match her earrings. With a smile that rearranged her wrinkles, she motioned for David and Abby to come in.

He kept his nose from wrinkling as the odors of old grease and fresh liniment hung in the air. It was the same smell that had filled the *dawdi haus* where his great-grandparents had lived during the earliest years of his childhood. He hadn't liked it then, but now found himself realizing how much he'd missed it after his parents had taken him far away from their family's home.

Odd how he'd forgotten about that until now. Every time he was with Abby, some aspect of his past seemed to sneak out from behind the walls he'd built around his memories. What bothered him was how many good memories he'd cast away along with the painful ones.

"No need for introductions," Doris said as she ushered them into the hallway that separated the front two rooms. "I've seen you around town since you were knee-high to a grasshopper, David, and Abby and I talked a few days ago. And you know who I am. I'm the only one here older than the mountains." Her laugh was a raspy chortle that invited him to join in.

He did, along with Abby, as they followed Doris into a crowded room that might once have been a dining room. A large table had been placed in the middle. Its legs appeared to be darkly stained maple, but the top was so covered with books and boxes and paper and stacks of other items he couldn't guess if it'd been made from the same type of wood.

The rest of the room was as overloaded. Chairs that must have been used with the table were mixed in with a pair of rockers and two overstuffed recliners. The drapes were pulled, keeping out the sunshine, but he thought he saw photographs or maybe paintings on the wall. One door, propped open with a brick at the bottom, led into the kitchen, which was, he was shocked to see, neat. Other than a canister set and a microwave, nothing was on any of the glistening counters.

"Go ahead," Doris said. "Say what everyone says."

"What's that?" David asked, edging between the table and one of the recliners so he could give Abby enough space to enter, too.

"That I need to have a yard sale and get rid of this junk."

"It doesn't look like junk to me." He lifted a basket from the table. "This is handwoven and it's old. It's got to be worth quite a bit of money."

Doris smiled at him as if he were the most wonderful person on the planet. "That's what

I've told folks, but all they see is the mess. They don't realize how long it took me and my husband to find these items." She crooked a finger. "Come over to this corner. It's where the sewing machine is."

Abby stayed back while David followed the old woman toward the farthest corner. It was a tight squeeze between the furniture and the various items stacked everywhere. He put his hand on a pile of records that reached almost to his waist. The top one was the Beatles' first album, and he wondered what other gems might be hiding in that mound.

"Here it is," trilled Doris as she flung out her hand like a ringmaster in a tiny circus.

He peered through the dusk and made out the shape of a shadowed treadle machine. He wasn't sure he would have been able to see it if he hadn't known what he was searching for.

"Do you mind if I open the drapes, so I can get a good look at it?" he asked.

"They don't open." Doris gave him an embarrassed smile. "The gizmo that moves them in the track broke a few years ago."

He smiled. "They come off their tracks pretty easily. I can check it and fix it for you, if you'd like."

"Go ahead and look at it, but I warn you. It's most likely broken. I gave it a big tug and I heard something snap." She looked at Abby.

"I'm not the most patient person in the world. You'd have thought years of teaching home ec would have taught me patience, but it seems to have done the opposite."

"What's home ec?" asked Abby.

"Home economics." The elderly woman smiled. "What you Amish, my dear, learn from your mothers and grandmothers as children. How to run a household, how to cook, how to clean and how to sew."

"There are classes for that in *Englisch* schools?"

"There were. I'm afraid the programs aren't what they used to be." Doris looked sad for a moment, but brightened. "What is? I'm not what I used to be, and neither is my old sewing machine. What do you think, young man? Do you think it can be fixed?"

"Anything can be fixed. All it takes is time and money."

"I don't have oodles of either." She winked at him.

David looked at the sewing machine. He guessed Doris had been quite the flirt in her younger years. Then he corrected himself. He'd never heard a whisper of scandal about Doris or her late husband. More likely, as an older woman, she enjoyed the chance to act a bit shocking and watch how people reacted.

"Then we should get started, shouldn't we?"

He grabbed a handful of the brown drapes and gave a quick jerk.

A blizzard of dust exploded around him. As he coughed and sneezed almost at the same time, his eyes burned. He squinted and realized the drapes were green beneath the thick layers of dust. Waving the dust away, he started to speak, but kept sneezing.

When a tissue was pressed into his hand, he was thrilled to discover it was damp. He dabbed at his eyes, hoping to ease that discomfort first. As soon as he could open them without pain, he pulled out his own handkerchief and blew his nose.

Solicitude filled Abby's voice. "Are you okay, David?"

"I will be." He looked through watery eyes at Doris's dismay. "You should have warned me your draperies were loaded."

His teasing comment eased her distress and Doris laughed. "Look at him, Abby! That's how *he* is going to look when he's old."

He understood when Abby slid past the piles of assorted items. When she warned him to put his hand up to his forehead, he did, and she reached up to brush dust from his hair. Bits of it drifted onto her *kapp*.

"Be careful. You're just transferring it from

me to you," he said, flicking dust off the white organdy.

"Don't worry. Everything is washable."

He was captured anew by her pretty eyes. As the rest of the world vanished, he savored the invisible thread between them. He thought of how they'd stood so close before, and how on each occasion it seemed as if the stolen moment lasted a lifetime and at the same time sped past so fast he didn't have a chance to grasp it.

The bridge between them collapsed when Doris called, "You'd better step out of the way, Abby, before he moves the other drape. There's a bunch of dust on it, too, I'm sure."

Blinking as if awaking from a sweet dream, Abby moved back from him. She bumped into the table and reached out to keep a half dozen metal pails from falling over. In the faint light, he could see how her cheeks had colored when Doris urged her to be careful.

"I'm sorry," Abby said.

"Don't apologize, my girl." The old woman sighed. "I should have emptied this room long ago, but I couldn't bring myself to throw out a single thing Arnie and I collected. This was his room, you know. The room where he displayed his favorite finds. After he retired and began attending auctions and flea markets almost every day, the room began to fill up. When I'm here with his special items, it's almost as if I can believe he's hiding behind one of the piles." She waved her hand at them. "Listen to me. I sound like a silly, old woman."

"No," said Abby as she edged over to Doris. "You sound like a woman who found the love of her life and knows how blessed she was."

"You're wise for such a young woman." She patted Abby's hand before adding, "Now, David, be careful with those drapes, so you don't end up sneezing again."

David heeded her warning. He drew aside the both sides with care and dropped the ends of the drapes over chairs to hold them open. The room brightened as the sunlight flowed through the window for the first time in what he guessed had been years. As he recalled, Arnie Blomgren had died around the time David was in fifth grade.

The sewing machine beside the window was dull with rust. The veneer on its case had been raised in several spots along the top, and one of the hinges on the top had lost two of its three screws, leaving the lid at an angle. The belt that should connect the treadle to the handwheel on the right side of the machine was lying in dusty black pieces on the floor. No needle was in place and the feeding mechanism set above the bobbin was as rusty as the table legs. However, the lettering for the manufacturer's name was bright, not a hint of the paint missing.

"It can be repaired, can't it?" the old woman asked. "It belonged to my grandmother first and then my mother and now me. I want to have it in working condition when I pass it along."

"It needs a lot of work, but we have volunteers who want to help us with it."

"Volunteers?" Doris scowled as she looked from him to Abby. "Exactly how many people are you planning to bring into my house?"

Abby saw David's shock at the old woman's abrupt, sharp question. When he sneezed again before he could answer, she jumped in. "Our volunteer youth group wants to do more than rebuild houses. They want to help others in town. I thought, after speaking with you, that the sewing machine might be the perfect project. It'll teach them about something they may never have encountered before. However, having them here is up to you."

Doris considered her words. "Will I be able to oversee them?"

"If you want to. It'll be *gut* for them to work with other adults, and I'm sure you have a lot to teach them. Like I said, it's up to you. If you don't want others here, David and I will make sure your treadle machine is fixed. I do hope you'll consider having the youth group involved."

The old woman looked around the room and a slow smile emerged across her face. "This old house has been silent for too long. It might do it—and me—some good to have youthful voices in here." She raised a single gnarled finger, wagging it first at Abby and then at David, who was struggling not to sneeze again. "They've got to be willing to learn what I can teach them."

"Home ec classes?" Abby asked as David dashed tears from his watery eyes and inched away from the sewing machine to join her and Doris at the other end of the table. "Cooking and sewing?"

"You can teach them about cooking, but I don't know many young people who understand how to sew on a button properly."

"A *gut* lesson for you to teach them, ain't so?" She glanced at David, urging him to join the conversation.

He gave her a quick nod. "That's a lesson I could use, too, Doris."

"Well, then, it's settled." The old woman led the way out of the crowded room into the entry hall.

Abby gasped when David stumbled into her. His arms wrapped around her and she fought to keep her knees from buckling. As swiftly as he'd grabbed her, he released her. His cheeks had become an attractive shade of red.

"Sorry," he said as he looked at the rag rug on the floor. "I caught my foot on it."

Doris tsk-tsked. "I thought I had that rug secured better. Wait a minute." She disappeared into the kitchen.

Abby knelt by the rug. It was stuck to the floor on the far side, but was loose enough to catch David's foot. "This is a tripping hazard."

"What do you—" He halted his own question as Doris returned.

"Here." She held out a roll of wide tape.

Abby recognized it as double-sided tape. She took the roll. "This should be only a temporary solution, Doris." She glanced at the wall behind the old woman. "What do you say to hanging the rug on the wall? It's way too pretty to be walked on."

"On the wall? Nonsense! It's an old rag rug I made out of even older rags. People would think I'm crazy if I hang that beat-up old rug on the wall like it was some fancy painting." She waved her hand toward the rug. "Tape it down and it'll stay in place."

"Please think about moving it. If you trip…"

"I didn't. Your young man did."

Wanting to argue further, Abby knew she risked alienating Doris. "You know what? This rug is the perfect size to put beneath the sewing machine while we're working on it. Don't you think so?"

David started to answer but she motioned him to silence. The response had to come from Doris.

Again the elderly woman thought about the question before she nodded. "That makes sense. If oil drips on it while you're getting the rust off, it won't ruin anything important. I can always make another rug if this one gets stained."

David pulled up the rug, leaving stickiness behind on the hardwood floor. He carried it into the overfilled room and lifted each corner of the treadle machine to put it beneath it.

Abby stood and took a step toward the kitchen. Doris halted her by saying, "Don't worry. My cleaning lady will get the excess glue off the floor when she comes tomorrow."

"And we'll be back next week with the teens," David said once he'd rejoined them in the hallway. "Is next Tuesday okay for you, Doris?"

"I should check my social calendar in case I'm entertaining the queen that afternoon." With a guffaw, Doris added, "Next Tuesday is fine."

Smiling as they bade the elderly woman goodbye, Abby went out with David. Neither of them spoke until they reached David's truck, which was covered with dirt and salt stains from driving during the winter.

"It's good to see," David said with a hushed chuckle, "that age hasn't slowed her down."

"She's a *wunderbaar* lady. *Danki* for agreeing to the project for the youth group." She drew her coat around her. Would spring ever get to Evergreen Corners?

"Helping those who need us is a lesson these kids have already learned, but now they can learn that those older than them have special skills to teach them." He looked past her to the house. "The sewing lessons will have to wait. The first thing the kids are going to have to do is move that stuff out of the dining room so we can get to the sewing machine."

"Wouldn't it be easier to move the sewing machine into the other front room?"

"Easier, maybe, but I don't know if, before it's stabilized, it could endure that journey."

She smiled. "You'll figure out something, David. Challenges don't seem to scare you, and I've got one for you."

"What's that?" He leaned his elbow on his truck.

"I'd like to get the kids involved in a special project before next week. What do you say to taking them on an outing on Saturday?"

"Where?"

"A hike."

He pushed away from the truck, his eyes wide with disbelief. "You want to hike up a mountain *now*?"

"Why not? The snow is gone."

"Here in the valley. There will be plenty of snow up at the top of the higher mountains."

"I wasn't thinking of a big mountain. More like a small one." She pointed to the gap where the road ran east and west through the valley. "Like that one. I asked around and I was told that there was an easy trail that should be passable to the top."

"That's Quarry Mountain." He put his hand up to shield his eyes. "It looks as if most of the snow is gone, but looks can be deceiving when it comes to mountains. The weather changes quickly up there."

She sighed. He had a rebuttal for everything she suggested. "Maybe it's a *dumm* idea. I thought it'd be fun for the kids. They're pretty down after their latest run-ins with Hunter and his cronies."

"It would be fun…in a few months."

"When the bugs are out?"

He smiled. "Okay, you've got me on that one. The bugs can be nasty once the weather is warm. Even this time of year, we'd need to make sure the kids put on bug repellent. Ticks don't take any time off."

"We want to give the youth group some time away, and what better way is there to do that than to get them up on a mountain where they can spend time with nature and God? It'll also give you a better chance to get to know the kids."

"I know most of them."

"True, but working together toward a common goal helps us see the truth about each other. It could be a lot of fun." The wrong word, she knew, when his smile slipped. She kept her own in place. "It'll also give you a chance to discover which kid has which skills that will be useful in fixing the sewing machine."

And for you and me to be together for a day. She held her breath as she waited for him to reply, hoping he couldn't discern the words she hadn't spoken.

"We'll give it a try…as long as the weather cooperates." He opened the passenger door. "I know you Amish prefer horses and buggies, but can I give you a ride to the community center?"

"Ja," she started to say. But as the image of the night when she hadn't let Bert Fetter take her home in his buggy exploded into her mind, she made some trite excuse about needing to run an errand on her way to the community center.

It wasn't a lie. She'd planned to stop at Pastor Hershey's house soon to talk to him about other ideas she had for the youth group.

David's eyes became hooded as he nodded. He closed the passenger door and walked around his truck. Getting in, he drove away without a wave.

She watched until the vehicle turned a corner. Then she began to walk toward the community center. A shiver that had nothing to do with the cold slid down her spine. Hadn't God wanted her to avoid following her heart, which brought trouble to her and others? Shouldn't it be second nature now to listen to common sense rather than what her heart yearned for?

It was becoming more obvious when she spent time with David that she hadn't learned a single thing.

Chapter Nine

On Saturday, bright sunshine woke Abby as it peeked around the shade on the window beside her bed. Sitting, she pulled up the shade and peeked out. The day looked beautiful, but she'd learned better than to trust how a day *looked*. Especially on a New England spring day when the weather changed more often than *Englisch* teens altered their hairstyles and colors.

Unlatching the window, she lifted it. A gentle breeze, cool but promising to grow warmer as the sun rose, drifted into her room, sweeping away the winter stuffiness. It made her want to jump to her feet and twirl around as she had when she was a little girl. There was something about the first days of spring, something so fresh, so precious, so fleeting, she could understand why the birds sang and the butterflies danced from flower to flower.

She let the curtains fall into place for privacy as she dressed for the day ahead. This was the day she and David were taking the teens up Quarry Mountain. Since their conversation in front of Doris's house, she hadn't spoken to him other than a quick greeting when he'd come to pick up Mikayla the next day. For the past two afternoons, Mikayla had been biking to and from the community center.

What would it be like when they spent time with the teens today? Anticipation made her clumsy and she spilled the milk and toast on the floor while making breakfast. Though her brother couldn't hide his curiosity about her uncharacteristic clumsiness, Isaac didn't ask what was bothering her. Instead he talked about the next foundation they must finish preparing, so the concrete could be poured on Monday morning.

One of the *Englischers* working with her brother came to the apartment to give them a ride. She'd be dropped off where the hikers would be meeting. He and Isaac then would head out of town to get more wood for the concrete forms. The trailhead wasn't more than a half mile out of their way.

She was the first to arrive at the parking area edged by thick trees. As she shrugged on the backpack with her hiking supplies, she urged the men to go ahead with their tasks. Isaac hesitated then nodded when she told him she'd wait at one of the picnic tables that gave her a view of the footbridge over the brook.

The truck left and she listened to the birds calling to one another. The trill of a cardinal and the more raucous cry of a blue jay both silenced as a hawk soared on the thermals high above the woods.

A few minutes later, another familiar truck pulled into the parking area. She raised her hand to wave to David and Mikayla, but paused when she saw only one person in it. Sliding off the picnic table, she waited while David parked the truck and got out. He slung a pack over one shoulder.

"Good morning," he said as he walked toward her.

She returned the greeting, then asked, "Where's Mikayla? She's coming, isn't she?"

"She is, but she wanted to ride her bike. She's decided she wants to enter a triathlon this summer."

Abby arched her brows. "That's quite a goal."

"If you ask me, her goal is to spend time out of the house."

She started to reply but he waved her to silence. With a sigh, he said, "Ignore me. We've had a few tough days."

"Is there anything I can do to help?"

"I'd say yes, if I knew what would help."

She put her hand on his arm. When he settled his fingers over hers, she wished she had the words to tell him everything would be fine. God had a plan for David and Mikayla, and only He could see what it was.

When she heard voices, she looked past David. Two people, one pushing a bike and one slowly driving a car, approached the parking lot. She stiffened when she recognized the car. It was the one she'd seen the night the bullies had taunted Reece. Her breath caught over her pounding heart when she realized the person with the bike was Mikayla.

Abby was racing across the parking lot before she'd come up with an idea of what to do or say. Before she could reach them, the car accelerated with the screech of tires. Hands seized her arms, jerking her aside as the car sped past her, so close its passing ruffled her heavy coat. She held her arm up over her face to protect it from the gravel spewing from the tires.

"Stupid kid," David snarled. "Are you okay?"

She nodded, then ran to Mikayla, who'd let her bike fall to the ground with a clang. Putting her arms around the girl, she held her while Mikayla wept. Abby wanted to offer solace, but any she could think of sounded trite even to her.

"Don't ask," Mikayla whispered as if Abby had spoken the banal phrases. "Please."

"He made you cry."

"Please let it go." She raised her head and dashed away the tears. "There's nothing you can do. Either of you."

Abby wished David would embrace his daughter, but he stood to one side, as unsure as she was about what to say. When she saw his hands were clenched at his sides, she hoped he wouldn't do anything foolish.

More vehicles pulled into the parking area, and Mikayla ran to join her friends.

"Don't worry," David said as he picked up the discarded bike. "I won't punch that kid's lights out, though I'm tempted. I wasn't raised to solve my problems by punching someone."

Relieved, Abby said, "There must be something we could do."

"If you figure out what it is, let me know." He didn't add more as he walked the bike to his truck and lifted it into the back, locking it in place so it wouldn't be stolen while they were hiking.

The kids—mostly *Englisch* except for the two plain teenagers, Dwight and Roy, who'd come to Evergreen Corners with Isaac—spilled out of the vehicles and grabbed their backpacks, flinging them over their shoulders as their parents urged them to have fun. While the other trucks and SUVs backed out of the parking lot, David made sure the hikers had put on bug spray before he checked each teen had brought everything on the supply list they'd been given the day the hike was announced.

Two boys forgot to bring extra bottles of water, and Cindi didn't have a second pair of socks. David pulled four bottles out and handed two to each of the boys while Mikayla found an extra pair of socks that would fit the girl.

Cindi wrinkled her nose when she saw they were simple white crew socks, but didn't say anything but thanks as she tucked them into her pack. Abby wanted to thank Mikayla. She didn't, not wanting to draw more attention to the girl who was acting as if she hadn't been crying minutes ago.

David led the way to the hiking trail. The kids motioned for Abby to follow. She'd planned on bringing up the rear, which would allow her to keep a *gut* eye on them, but she realized she had to trust the teens when she saw how they drew Mikayla into their midst. Her concerns were eased when she realized David's daughter's attempt to hide her tears from her friends had failed.

Abby caught up with him and began the slow, steady walk up Quarry Mountain. It didn't take long before isolated clumps of snow beneath the trees began to connect together like bubbles of mercury condensing into a puddle. Abby discovered what looked like snow was closer to ice. The tops of the snow piles had melted and refrozen over and over into miniature glaciers.

"Watch where you walk," she cautioned, though it wasn't necessary. The kids from Evergreen Corners had been climbing the sides of these mountains their whole lives. The plain teens were already being careful.

The path led them among tall trees and around raw ridges of rock that rose in front of them like ancient walls. Each time they stepped around one, Abby longed to pull her coat closer. The wind seemed to be waiting to ambush them on the far side of each outcropping.

"I think it's getting colder with each step we take," she said.

"Just your imagination." David laughed. "What would your pioneer ancestors say if they saw you now?"

"That I was foolish to leave the indoor comforts they couldn't have envisioned."

His laugh soared at her sour tone, and she smiled. She liked the sound of his laughter, probably because she heard it so seldom.

A tiny waterfall, no wider than her shortest finger, dropped over layers of stone to fall into a pool edged with last fall's leaves. Everything glistened as if covered with a thin sheet of ice, but the plants around the pool were only wet.

"Watch your step." David took her hand and led her around the pool.

When he continued to hold it as they climbed the ever steeper path, she knew she should draw away. She couldn't force her fingers to slip out of his. He withdrew his to pull aside a branch to let them pass, and she wished she could devise a way for him to hold her hand again.

The teens' voices grew quieter as they continued ascending through the thickening woods. She wasn't sure if it was because they were awed by nature's beauty or if the steep path was leaving them short of breath. David walked ahead with a slow, steady pace and called for breaks to hydrate every twenty minutes.

After the second stop among the trees that hid the other mountains and the valley from them, Abby dropped back to walk with Mikayla. The other kids surged to catch up with David, giving them a moment of privacy.

"How are you doing?" Mikayla asked before Abby could speak.

"I'm discovering muscles I never knew I had in flat Lancaster County." She laughed. "I'll have a chance to use my *grossmammi*'s surefire muscle liniment tomorrow."

"Better use it tonight before your muscles

cramp up more." A faint smile pulled at Mikayla's lips. "I've learned that the hard way since beginning my training for the race." Pausing as she walked around a boulder that split the path, she said, "I've been thinking about Mrs. Blomgren. Do you think she's going to be alone for Easter?"

"I don't know. I thought you said she was Jack's great-*aenti*. Will his family be going to her house that day?"

Mikayla shrugged. "Maybe, but it would be sad if she's alone."

"It would." She watched the girl's face, which never hid her emotions.

Now Mikayla was wrestling with the problem of making sure Doris had a memorable Easter. Abby didn't say anything, waiting to discover what solution the girl would find.

"Y'know," Mikayla said, looking at the path ahead of them as her thin smile returned, "Dad and I always exchanged decorated eggs on Easter morning. My first one ended up in pieces because I'd tried to paint it with a crayon. Later on, I learned how to dye them and put pictures on the eggs. I cut them out of magazines and catalogs, and I tried to find pictures that would remind him of something fun we'd done in the past year. Mine got to be as fancy as the ones he made." Her smile faded as she said, "I'm going to miss doing that this year."

"You don't have to stop doing it. There must be someone who'd love an egg you decorated."

"You mean David?" She shook her head. "He's too serious. He wouldn't find it as funny as my dad did when I gave him an egg with silly pictures on it."

"Think about it, Mikayla. There must be someone who'd love to get an Easter egg from you."

"Maybe Mrs. Blomgren!"

"That's a *wunderbaar* idea. You could talk to Jack about it and maybe he'd like to make one for her, too."

Mikayla shook her head. "It's *my* family's special tradition. I'm not sure I want to share it."

Abby nodded. Though she knew how much it would mean to David for his daughter to give him a special egg and include him in that precious tradition, she must be careful. Following her heart had wreaked havoc in too many lives already.

More than an hour later, they reached the top of Quarry Mountain. The forest opened and they had a magnificent view of the valley and the twisting path of Washboard Brook through its center.

A cheer rose from the teens when Reece pulled out his cell phone and motioned for the others to gather around a marker at the top. It identified the nearby mountains and villages. The *Englisch* kids rushed to crowd in around it for the selfie.

"Abby? David? Aren't you coming?" Jack shouted. He waved to the plain teens. "C'mon, guys. Don't you want to be in the picture?"

"Not me." Abby took a half step back. Glancing at Dwight and Roy, she saw their relief that she'd spoken up, saving them from having to do so. "We Amish don't get photographed."

"Why?" asked Lily as she sat on the slanting surface of the marker. The redhead was as close to Jack as possible. Abby guessed her participation in the group was because of her crush on him.

"We're taught it goes against God's commandment to make any graven images."

The *Englisch* kids exchanged uneasy looks, and she realized they'd come to accept her as just another volunteer. Maybe Isaac was right that she was spending too much time with *Englischers*.

Mikayla's soft voice broke the silence. "That's from the ten commandments. The second commandment, so it must have been a big deal to God."

Reece looked at his phone and started to put it in his pocket. "I'm sorry, Abby, Roy, Dwight. We didn't mean to make you uncomfortable."

"You didn't make us uncomfortable," Abby hurried to reassure him. "Go ahead and take your picture." She tapped her bonnet. "I've already put the image of you dancing around the top of the mountain right here. I've learned to keep my memories close so I can enjoy them, and I'm going to have lots of great memories of this hike."

She watched the teens take their photos before finding rocks to sit on as they pulled out their lunches and water bottles. Glad to see that Roy and Dwight settled in for the lunch right along with the teens from Evergreen Corners, she relaxed. Everyone had been honest when they'd said they hadn't meant to make anyone else feel ill at ease.

David walked over. "Is this rock taken?" He pointed to her left.

"I was saving it for you."

"It doesn't look comfortable."

"Beggars can't be choosers, or so I've heard."

Again he chuckled, and again she savored the sound. Like seeing the kids exultant at reaching the top of the mountain, his laugh would be a memory she'd pull out later to enjoy over and over.

"You handled that picture issue well," he said as he opened the bag containing a turkey sandwich.

"Plain people have to walk a fine line between the *Englisch* world and our own. We believe we shouldn't play a large part in worldly matters, but it's impossible not to find ourselves in your world at times like this." She opened her own lunch bag and pulled her feet up on the rock. "In order to help those in need, it's necessary that we live among you."

"Yet tomorrow you and the other Amish volunteers will worship alone."

She grinned as she corrected, "We will worship together while you attend your own services. God listens to each of us when we gather into our congregations."

"You seem so sure of that."

Reaching for a potato chip, she halted as she asked, "Aren't you?"

"I try to be, but I find doubts creeping in sometimes."

"It's okay to have doubts. We're imperfect humans, so our faith is imperfect, too. Only God is perfection." She took a bite of the chip, then said, "I try to remind Isaac of that when he becomes too focused on getting everything perfectly right and becomes impossible to be around."

David unscrewed the top of his water bottle. "You love your brother, don't you?"

"Sometimes more than others." She laughed. "Isaac wants so much to avoid making mistakes."

"Don't we all?" His gaze crossed the mountaintop to where Mikayla was perched on a flat-topped boulder between Reece and Dwight. "I'd like to know the right way to reach her."

"Let me tell you something my *daed* used to say. Teenagers are like onions."

He gave her a lopsided grin. "Do you mean because they can smell bad?"

"No, I mean they're like onions because they have layers hidden one within another. If you look at them, you see a thin skin, but not inside."

"And if you delve too deeply, you can end up crying." He sighed as he stared off into the trees. "You've cut them, and tears fall."

"Exactly."

His gaze focused on her again. "How did you get to be an expert on teens?"

"Through trial and error." She smiled. "A lot of error."

"Now *that* I understand."

She resisted reaching out to pat his hand. If she touched him again, she wasn't sure if she could persuade her fingers ever to let go. She wanted to help David and Mikayla, but listening to her heart, which urged her to jump in with both feet, might be the very thing that destroyed whatever chances they had to become a family. She couldn't risk heeding her heart.

Not now when the stakes were so high.

David wasn't surprised when Abby changed the subject. Why would she want to be encased in his dreariness? If he'd chosen to prove to her that Chelsea had been right when she'd said he was no fun, then he was doing a great job.

Finishing his lunch, he stood. His leg muscles protested and he winced. He'd considered himself in good shape, but he hadn't been ready for a long hike after a sedentary winter. He heard muttering from the teens as they got up, too.

"Just think," he called out to them as he shoved his lunch bag into his backpack and pulled out an unopened bottle of water. "We'll be using a different set of muscles going down the mountain."

That brought a new round of groans, but the kids were eager to see what awaited them on the far side of the mountain. Not that they'd discover anything new. They'd been up and down the highway that cut across Vermont. The view from the mountain's side should be quite different from what they saw along the road.

The teens regained their good humor as they started on the path to the neighboring valley. Stopping for lunch had revitalized them, and they teased each other in between singing songs that matched their pace down the mountain. David let them take the lead and hung back to walk with Abby.

She didn't speak, and neither did he as he took in the amazing vista in front of them. From up on the mountain, the extent of the damage from the flood was visible, but he didn't focus on that. Instead he watched dark-colored birds gliding through the sky. He squinted, wondering if they might be bald eagles hunting in the lake north of the village. Without binoculars, he couldn't be certain. The kids pointed out the birds, and he guessed they shared his hope that eagles floated above them.

They were halfway down the mountain when he called for a rest. As he opened his water bottle, he asked, "See the steam, Abby? Look to the left of it. Can you see a sugarhouse down there among the trees?"

She squinted. "A sugarhouse? Oh, maple syrup!"

"It's one of the products Vermont is known for. That and snow."

"And ice cream and cheese."

He grinned. "Spoken like a true Vermont dairy farmer."

"That's what my family is now. Vermont dairy farmers."

"Including you?"

"I will be once I return home. Nobody escapes barn chores in my family."

His smile wobbled as she spoke of leaving Evergreen Corners. It was inevitable, and he knew it was for the best. That didn't halt the pain piercing his heart.

He was saved from having to come up with

a reply when Jack sprinted over to them and urged, "Let's go visit the sap house! It'll be fun."

"We told your parents we'd have you down the mountain at three. They'll worry if we're late."

"Come on. It'll be fun."

From behind him, he heard Mikayla mutter, "He doesn't ever want to have fun."

Shock riveted him as her words echoed what he'd heard when Chelsea dumped him. The fifteen years collapsed into a single second, and he could recall his soon-to-be ex-girlfriend walking out after she'd told him that she wanted to have fun. Lots of it. Without him.

Was that really how his daughter thought of him, too?

Not any longer!

"Anyone got a decent signal on their cell phone?" David asked and saw Abby smile at him.

Cindi and Mikayla each had a couple of bars, so he set them to contacting the parents and Isaac, who was responsible for the plain teens, to let them know the kids would be an hour later than planned. The parents agreed to meet the kids at the sap house.

David wondered if something sweet was the lure that sent the kids at a faster pace down the mountain. They reached the bottom and crossed the road to the sap house in less than half the time he'd expected.

The sap house, set in the shadow of some tall pines, was about the size of a pair of one-car garages set back-to-back. Made of logs covered with bark, it had a door at the front. A couple of windows broke the long expanse on the sides. In front of a second building, which had big front windows, was the parking lot. Signs hanging from the other building identified it as a gift shop.

"Watch where you're walking," he warned. "There's plastic tubing running out to the sugar bush. Take a minute and look. You'll see the sap coming into the sap house."

Squatting as if they were little kids, the teens watched the sap slide through the tubes. When a dead bug slipped past in a tube, there was a combination of laughter and disgust. They were assured no insects went into the syrup, but they kept jesting about maple syrup being a good source of protein.

"I've never seen these tubes up close before," Abby said.

"Syrup is big business in Vermont. The traditional taps, which are metal spigots driven into the maple trunks, are used by private individuals who get sap from a few trees. People producing lots of syrup have changed to this system. The sap is vacuumed out of the tree before being sent to the sap house."

"It doesn't hurt the trees?"

He smiled, not surprised her gentle heart was touched by the possible plight of maple trees. "There are studies going on to find that out, but for now, it doesn't seem to be having an impact on the trees. You can be certain the smart syrup producer wants to protect his sugar bush."

Herding the kids ahead of him toward the gift shop, he watched them go inside to the counter, where they could buy treats. The man behind the counter took orders for what was listed as maple snow.

"It's not snow." He gave them a slow wink. "There's not a lot of clean snow now, so we use shaved ice for our maple cones."

David helped Abby hand small paper cones to the teens. She had such an easy way with them, teasing and laughing along with the kids. They adored her, and it was simple to see why. When she spoke to them, she acted as if each teen was the most important person in the world. They crowded around her.

Not all of them.

Mikayla sat alone by the door.

"Go ahead," Abby murmured without looking at him. "She needs a cone, too."

Did she have eyes in the back of her head, or could she guess what he was thinking? He wasn't sure which possibility was more unsettling. If he went over, would Mikayla welcome him or not? Recalling how Abby had urged him to look on the positive side with his daughter rather than assume the negative, he took the cone she held out to him.

Sitting beside Mikayla, he held out the cone. She took it with a hushed, "Thank you."

He ate his own and hoped she'd say something else. She didn't, so before the silence grew too oppressive, he asked, "Do you like it?"

"Yes."

Instead of letting her terse answer put him off again, he said, "Me, too. I think the shaved ice is a nice contrast to the syrup."

"You do?" She looked at him directly as she seldom did. Surprise filled her eyes, and he guessed she hadn't expected him to say more after she'd tried to put an end to the conversation with her truncated response. Her eyes shifted to her cup as she added in a gentler tone, "I do, too."

"Sweet ending to a nice day. I'm glad you guys suggested we stop here."

A faint smile brushed her lips. "Me, too."

He considered saying something else, but didn't when a couple of the other teens joined them. Listening to them chatter, he scooped the last of the maple syrup from the paper cone. Mikayla listened more than she spoke.

Was she normally shy and quiet?

He searched his memory, as he had so many times, but couldn't pull up a single recollection of any conversations with her while her father was alive. Then, for the first time, he tried to remember how many times he'd witnessed Mikayla gabbing with her father.

Amazement struck him like a bolt of lightning as he couldn't recall a single time Mikayla had ever said more than a few words while he was present. He couldn't remember a single time when Boyd, like many other fathers, complained about his daughter babbling on and on about something that interested her.

Had he built up an image of what he'd assumed his life with a teen would be without considering the specific person involved? He didn't want to think that he'd let his own grief prevent him from seeing the reality right in front of him.

Abby joined them as vehicles pulled into the parking lot outside. The teens' parents had arrived. As the kids thanked him and Abby for the hike, he couldn't stop smiling. It'd gone so much better than he'd hoped, especially the last ten minutes when he'd had an actual conversation with his daughter.

"Didn't it go well?" Abby asked as they paid for the cones.

"Better than I'd hoped."

"I'm glad to hear that. Really glad." She

walked beside him outside, where the teens were as loud as the crows cawing in the trees. "*Boppli* steps are unsteady ones, but they take us where we need to go."

"*Boppli?*"

"Sorry. I should have said 'baby steps.' You understand some *Deitsch*, so I forget you don't know the language."

"I now know what I've gotten through osmosis from being around you Amish folks."

"Now?"

He struggled not to scowl at his own unthinking comment. Because he was happy Mikayla hadn't cut him off with a single-word reply wasn't an excuse for revealing too much to Abby. She was suspicious, and he couldn't blame her. His excuse had sounded feeble to his own ears. Would she let the whole matter go?

Unlikely, because her kind heart would urge her to find out what was bothering him so she could offer him help as she did everyone else. He needed to find a way to divert her curiosity without piling a layer of lies on the half-truths he'd lived with since he was a child.

Chapter Ten

After breakfast on Tuesday, Abby took the grease drawer outside. It was kept next to the griddle on the larger stove. Grease and debris were scraped into it each time someone cooked another batch of eggs or bacon or pancakes. Keeping the griddle clean made the food taste better, but the drawer had to be emptied once each meal was over.

Her nose wrinkled as she carried it to the grease barrel behind the kitchen. Though they dumped it twice a day, the used grease reeked. She opened the barrel while balancing the drawer with care. Using a long spatula to slide the grease and food out of the drawer, she made sure the drawer didn't fall into the barrel. She'd done that once and learned her lesson after spending hours washing grease off the stainless-steel drawer.

That was a lesson she didn't need to be taught a second time.

As she closed the grease barrel and made sure it was secure so wandering bears, hungry after their winter hibernation, couldn't force it open and make a mess of the whole parking lot, she paused and looked down the hill. Listening to the birds and smiling when she saw a full-chested robin hunting in the grass, she watched the water in Washboard Brook tumble over the rocks.

A phone rang in the distance, but she ignored it. The men working on the house rebuilding sites wouldn't be ready for their midmorning *kaffi* for another hour. They were the only ones who called the community center. Everyone else contacted the secretary at the chapel.

She took in a deep breath. If she spread her arms, could she take off like the birds and soar through the early-spring morning? Laughing at her folly, she grimaced when she saw the grease staining her hands. She'd better wash it off right away.

When she went inside, Abby propped open the door to let in the fresh breezes, but had to close it after too many bugs decided to come in. What they needed was a screen door. That way the wood door could be left open to let air circulate through the kitchen. She would ask Pastor

Hershey if there were screens for the door and windows. Soon they would be roasted as much as the food if they couldn't open up the kitchen and let fresh air in.

Would she be in Evergreen Corners by the time summer arrived?

She sighed. After their worship service on Sunday, she'd heard Dwight and Roy talking about how they'd be finishing their time in the village at month's end. Isaac had hinted she should leave in the hired van with them. She'd told him she couldn't go while she was helping with the youth group. Her brother had said he'd talk to Glen about the program and see what could be done.

Why did Isaac have to be so insistent that he knew best for her? She was taking care to do what needed to be done instead of what her heart longed to do. He couldn't be upset about her relationship with David. She hadn't seen David since he and Mikayla, along with Reece, had stopped to visit Doris yesterday. The old woman had welcomed them like long-lost family and Abby had realized anew how lonely she must be.

She looked up when the door to the street opened. Glen walked in, and her heart clenched. Was he coming to tell her that she should go home as Isaac wanted?

Then she noticed he was with a woman whose head reached as high as his shoulder. On her shiny black hair, she wore a *kapp* pleated in a box shape. Her black apron over a pale blue dress made parts of her disappear into the shadows as they crossed the room.

"I've brought you some new help," Glen announced with his usual smile. "We've got a bunch of new volunteers, so we can start the next three houses soon. By the way, this is Rachel Yoder. Rachel, this is Abby. She can show you around the kitchen and get you started."

Greeting the woman who looked to be in her thirties, Abby waved to Glen as he left to deal with one of the other dozens of issues he had to handle each day. Glad Glen hadn't mentioned a word about Abby giving up the youth group, she gave Rachel a quick tour of the kitchen, interspersing her descriptions of what they did and when with questions about the newcomer.

Abby learned Rachel was from Maine. Rachel was a widow who had come to Evergreen Corners with her young daughters. She'd left them at the day care center that had moved from the community center to a nearby church basement a couple of months ago.

"You'll find folks in Evergreen Corners are welcoming," Abby said with a smile after she'd offered Rachel *kaffi*.

Taking the cup with a shy smile, Rachel said, "I've already seen that. We arrived less than two hours ago, and we already have a place to stay and my *kinder* are being cared for while I work. What do you want me to do first?"

"Why don't you—" Abby flinched when the phone by the back door rang.

It startled Rachel, too, because she stiffened and looked in every direction until her gaze alighted on the phone.

"Wait a sec. I should get that." Glancing at the clock, Abby frowned. Who was calling at this hour? Maybe one of the other volunteers couldn't come in today. She ignored her guilt that she might have ignored the call from an ill person when she was outside earlier.

"Abby?" came the response to her hello.

"David?" she asked, astonished. She blurted out her first thought. "Is Mikayla okay?"

"She's fine, but I need you to come over to Doris's house right away."

"What's happened?"

"Get over here. I'll explain when you get here."

She started to ask another question, then heard other voices in the background. Did they belong to the teen group? No, that was impossible. The kids were in school on a Tuesday morning, so they wouldn't have gone to Doris's house until their classes were over.

The phone went dead. David had hung up. What was going on?

Pausing long enough to tell Rachel that she had to leave and to begin making sandwiches for lunch with the leftover beef in the fridge, Abby pulled on her coat and bonnet. She was glad for her sneakers as she ran down the side of the village green toward the short street where Doris Blomgren lived. Each time her feet struck the sidewalk, fear rammed through her.

God, watch over us. The prayer repeated in her head on an endless loop.

As she hurried along the slate sidewalk on Doris's street, she gasped. Doris's house looked deserted. No motion was visible beyond the sheer curtains crisscrossing the tall windows, not even the flicker from the TV.

She raced up the steps and across the porch. She was reaching for the bell when the door was flung open. David, his coat half-unzipped, motioned for her to come in.

"What's wrong, David? You look pale. Are you sick?"

"I'm fine, and everything is okay now. The rescue squad just left."

The rescue squad was what the locals called their volunteer EMTs. "Why were they here?"

He wiped his hands on the dish towel he'd tucked into the waist of his jeans. "Doris fell sometime during the night."

"Oh, my! How's she doing?" She turned in both directions, hoping for a glimpse of the elderly woman.

"She's at the hospital. The EMTs are transporting her there."

"And you're doing dishes?"

He shook his head. "I've been cleaning up while I waited for you to get here."

"Waiting? You just called."

"I tried calling a few times before, and I didn't get any answer."

"I was outside." She began to explain about emptying the grease drawer.

He interrupted her. "Doris hit her head when she fell." He sighed. "She tried to crawl to the phone before she collapsed. I found her less than a foot from it."

Abby put her hands over her mouth to silence her gasp of dismay at the thought of the kind woman suffering such an injury. When David put his fingers on her arm, she looked up at him and saw her distress mirrored in his eyes.

"You found her?" she whispered.

"Yes." His voice was clipped, as if he feared he would be sick to his stomach at any minute. "I stopped to make sure I had the tools we were going to need for working this afternoon on her sewing machine. I found her in the hallway." He stepped aside and pointed at a rag rug half in and half out of the living room. It wasn't the same one they'd moved last week. "She must have put this one down in place of the rug I slipped under the sewing machine. I think it slid out from beneath her and sent her flying."

Abby started to nod, then gasped again. "You *think*? Didn't she tell you?"

"She wasn't conscious when I got here. By the time the rescue squad team was putting her into the ambulance, she'd opened her eyes, but she wasn't making much sense. She lost quite a bit of blood." He looked down at the floor. "And *that* was what I've been cleaning up."

She didn't hesitate. She flung her arms around his shoulders. "Oh, David! I'm so sorry you had to be the one to find her."

"I thank God I found her when I did. Who knows what might have happened by the time we arrived this afternoon?" His arm curved around her, keeping her close.

Leaning her head against his chest, she listened to the firm thump of his heart. It escalated when her cheek touched his coat. Warnings filled her head. Warnings that following her heart instead of what she should do would lead to disaster. She would listen to them…in a moment. For now, she savored drawing in the scent of his soap and whatever he'd used as after-shave.

Abby wasn't sure which one of them stepped back first.

David looked into the cluttered dining room. "I'd better head over to the hospital to see how she's doing."

She wasn't fooled by his nonchalant tone. He remained as upset over Doris's fall as she was. She tried to emulate his calm demeanor. "Do you mind if I tag along with you?"

"No. In fact, I was hoping you'd ask." A will-o'-the-wisp of a smile fled across his lips before he became serious again.

The faint change in his face generated an answering warmth deep within her where the coldest core of her fear cramped every breath she took. It wasn't much, but at the moment, it was more than enough.

The regional hospital, a building that looked as if it'd been added onto dozens of time in a hodgepodge of design, was filled with hushed urgency. David had sensed it the moment he and Abby walked through the automatic doors. He gritted his teeth as he waited with her by the elevator. The last time he'd been in this hospital had been the night of Boyd's accident. At

least, today, they hadn't had to come through
the emergency room, where the fight against
death was more dire and immediate.

He and Abby had stopped at the information desk and learned they'd be allowed to visit
Doris. It hadn't been the same the night Boyd
died. David hadn't had a chance to see him until
the funeral because nobody had been allowed
into the curtained space where his friend had
been taken. It'd taken hours to discover Boyd
was dead and more time to convince the staff
that the now-orphaned Mikayla shouldn't be left
alone in another section of the emergency room.

With effort, he shook those horrible memories from his head as one of the six elevators
pinged and the green up arrow over its door lit.
He stepped to the side as a man and a couple
of women, wearing white coats and talking in
hushed tones, emerged. Holding the door while
Abby entered, he punched the button for the
third floor.

"It must be a *gut* thing that she can have visi-
tors," Abby said over the piped-in music as the
elevator began a slow climb.

"You're probably right."

"Stop it!" she ordered, putting her fingers on
his arm.

"What?" He was amazed she'd touched him
again. Amish women didn't do such things with

an *Englischer*. What astonished him more was how the casual touch sent a flood of sweet sensation dancing across his skin. As it had when she'd given him that unexpected hug.

"Stop blaming yourself for what's happened."

"I'm not blaming myself."

"No? You aren't thinking about Doris as well as your friend's death?"

He stared at her. "Do you read minds?"

"No." She gave him a sad smile. "I do read faces, and yours is as easy to read right now as a large-print book. David, you must hand your guilt over to God. He had a reason for choosing you to be where you were both that night and today."

"I wouldn't have minded if He'd selected someone else."

The elevator lurched, and Abby's green eyes became almost perfect circles. Her fingers on his arm tightened when the car stopped and the lights flickered.

He waited a few seconds, then a few more, as the lights kept going on and off. The music jumped around like a record with a skip in it. Hearing the squeal of an emergency bell, he guessed someone in another elevator had pushed the call button.

Deciding he should do the same, he heard a

voice through the speaker. "Please stay where you are—"

"As if we have any choice," he whispered to Abby.

When she smiled in the faint glow from the emergency lights, he gave her a grin in return.

"There's been a power surge," continued the voice, "but we're getting the systems back online. You should be moving in a few sec—"

The car bounced once, then a second time, as the lights returned to full strength. It began to move again.

David grinned when Abby sent up a prayer of thanksgiving. He added an *amen* when she finished. He said nothing more when the car stopped and a ding announced they'd reached their floor. The doors slid open. He motioned for her to lead the way out.

She did quickly. As the doors closed again behind him, she said, "I've got an idea. Let's take the stairs down."

"Sounds like the best idea I've heard all day."

A stop at the nurses' station gave them directions to Doris's room. It was halfway down the hall on the right. The beep of machines and the hushed squeak of sneakers on the tiled floor was topped by quiet voices and the sounds of televisions in the rooms they passed.

David paused in the doorway and looked to

the bed on the right side of the curtain. Doris was lying with her eyes closed while a young man put a tray with her lunch on the table beside the bed. He nodded to David and Abby as he slipped by them on his way out the door.

Tiptoeing, David led Abby toward the bed. He didn't want to wake Doris if she was able to get some rest. Other than a pair of small bandages near shaved spots on her head, she looked unchanged.

The old woman's eyes popped open. "Oh, it's you! At least you don't want to drain me of blood or poke something into some part of my body." She raised her bed up into a sitting position.

"How are you feeling?" Abby asked.

"I don't know why they're keeping me here," the feisty woman complained. "I've told them I've been fine in that house for the past sixty-five years."

"You know," David said, "they won't let you go until they're satisfied you won't fall again."

She rolled her eyes as if she were no older than Mikayla. "David Riehl, I don't need you parroting to me what those doctors and nurses say. My knees may be giving out, but my ears and eyes are—praise the good Lord—working fine. I wish I could say the same for the rest of you."

"We want to keep you safe."

"I simply tripped on that stupid rag rug." She glanced at Abby and gave her a wry smile. "I should have listened to you, young lady, instead of worrying about my hardwood floors and the dirt brought in during mud season. If I had, I wouldn't be a prisoner in a hospital gown. I'm glad my Arnie isn't here to see me looking like this." Her smile widened. "I made sure I had makeup on every morning before he came down for breakfast. I wanted him always to see me at my best. You know? He won my heart by telling me I was the most beautiful girl he'd ever met, so I was determined he'd never have a reason to rue saying those words."

"I'm sure he thought you were beautiful, no matter what makeup you wore," David said as tears welled in Doris's eyes.

"I know the truth!" She wagged a finger at him, then pointed to Abby. "I was never as pretty as she is. She might be the most beautiful girl on God's green earth. I know you've got eyes in your head, David Riehl, so you've got to agree."

He glanced at Abby, who was blushing. He had to admit she was lovely, even without a hint of cosmetics to enhance her green-gray eyes. Wisps of honey-blond hair had escaped from her *kapp* to twist like corkscrews along both sides of her face. However, she must marry an Amish man, not David Riehl.

When Doris's eyelids became heavy, he and Abby turned to leave. Doris called them back and demanded they find out when she could get out of the hospital.

"I'm not sure if the staff will tell us anything," Abby said. "We're not your family."

"You're as close as I've got at the moment." She shut her eyes again, clearly believing the matter was settled.

Arching a brow at Abby, David walked with her into the hallway and to the nurses' desk.

A tall woman with a name tag that said Marilyn stood behind the counter. She smiled as they approached. "Can I help you?"

"We're friends of Doris Blomgren," he said. "She asked us to check when she'll be released."

"Your names?"

He gave them to the nurse and added, "I was the one who found her and called the rescue squad."

"Then you know she was unconscious. Until it can be determined whether that was the cause or the result of her fall, we won't release her."

"I agree," David said. "I'm sure Abby agrees, too."

Abby nodded. "Everyone agrees except Doris."

"She has a great-niece who's supposed to

be coming later today," Marilyn said. "We'll give her the facts, and she'll need to help Mrs. Blomgren decide where she can live now."

"You mean she won't be able to go home?" asked Abby.

"That's for the family to decide."

David saw Abby's shock, and he understood. Plain people kept their aged relatives near them. He recalled the *dawdi haus* where his great-grandparents had lived. It'd been connected by a breezeway to the main house where his grandparents and his father's unmarried siblings filled its many rooms. How many of them were still in that house? He hadn't thought about his aunts and uncles in years.

He thanked Marilyn for the information and, putting his hand on Abby's elbow, steered her away from the nursing station. Abby hesitated a moment and looked over her shoulder.

"This may be one time when you can't fix everything, Abby," he said.

"I can pray."

He flashed her a sad smile. "I suspect you've been doing that already."

"*Ja*, of course. My initial prayers were answered when I walked into Doris's room and saw her looking so much like her normal self. *Danki*, David, for caring enough to check at her house today. If you hadn't…"

She didn't finish, and she didn't have to. He'd had similar thoughts while waiting for the ambulance to arrive.

Neither of them said anything more as they went down the stairs and left the hospital. The silence wasn't oppressive, and he knew the near tragedy had drawn them closer together. He couldn't stop thinking of how right she'd felt in his arms.

Somehow he needed to find a way to turn off those thoughts.

Chapter Eleven

Two days later, Abby closed Doris Blomgren's front door behind her and smiled with relief. The elderly woman had been released from the hospital and her great-niece, Barbara, had come to oversee the house during Doris's recovery.

Abby had liked Barbara immediately. She was a younger version of Doris, and her *gut* sense of humor and no-nonsense demeanor would be an asset during the weeks ahead. Though Doris insisted she would be fine in no time, she was far from steady on her feet. Not only could Barbara help her deal with her new walker, but she would also make sure Doris took her pills. As the *doktor* had told them, a single mistake with her heart medicines could lead to another fall, and that fall might be fatal.

Doris had insisted Abby say nothing about the treadle sewing machine and David's plans to oversee the teens repairing it. The elderly woman wanted the working machine to be a surprise—and now a *danki*—for Barbara. It was a *wunderbaar* idea, and Abby had been delighted when Doris had shared her plans while Barbara was out of the room.

Before she'd left, Abby had promised Doris that the youth group would return to begin work as soon as Doris was allowed to have company. She had a project to work on with the teens until then, and she was anxious to discover what they thought of her idea. If it went as she hoped, she could share the story of the teens' efforts with Doris and see the old woman smile.

The sun was shining and Abby's steps were jaunty as she climbed the hill toward the community center. She could hear the staccato beat of nail guns and the shrill whine of power saws closer to the brook. Her steps faltered. In the not too distant future, she wouldn't have any excuse to remain in Evergreen Corners.

No, she wasn't going to think of that today. She had plenty of reasons to be in the village, and they weren't excuses so she could spend time with David and the teens.

Get out of my head, Isaac. Her brother hadn't bugged her again about heading home when he left in a few weeks. Had Glen convinced him that her help was important? Maybe Isaac had finally accepted she could be as stubborn as he was.

Several women, including Rachel, were busy in the kitchen when Abby walked in. She waved to them and then focused on the main room. She had a lot of work to do before the teens arrived after school. Hearing a sliding door on a van open behind the building, she smiled. Today should be an interesting one.

By midafternoon, everything was ready, and she was sure it was going to be fun. Abby watched as the teens arrived and approached the tables where she'd placed sewing machines she'd borrowed from the high school. The kids acted as skittish as if they were slipping into cages filled with wild man-eating tigers.

She hid her smile at the thought. Not giving any sign she'd expected them to be astonished by the activity she'd planned, she led the way to the tables.

"I thought we'd do something different today." She allowed herself a smile. "As you know, we were supposed to go to Doris Blomgren's house today and begin repairing her old sewing machine."

"How is she?" asked Lily, for once not focused on Jack.

"She's, as they say, resting comfortably. She won't be up to having guests for at least a couple of weeks. Until then, I thought we'd work on some projects in her honor."

"Like what?" Cindi frowned at the sewing machines. "Those look older than the hills."

"Not quite that old. They used to be part of the home economics classes Doris taught at the high school. When the program was cut, the machines were put in storage. Glen found them, and David oiled them before they were delivered here, so they're ready to go."

"Go where?" asked Roy, always the most literal one.

Abby laughed. "Go to work. In honor of Doris, I thought I'd give you some of the lessons she used to teach in her home ec classes."

"I thought home ec was cooking." Mikayla hung her coat on a hook and inched toward the closest machine, bending to peer at it with curiosity.

"Not from what Doris has told me." She glanced at each of the teens in turn. "We Amish don't have home ec courses in our schools. We girls learn to cook from our *mamms* and *grossmammis*."

"Not the boys?" Reece asked.

"Nah, they do the dishes," retorted Cindi.

"No, we don't." Dwight stuffed his hands into his pockets. "We do barn chores and work in the fields while the women handle the cooking and cleaning."

Cindi frowned. "Can't girls help with chores?"

"Anytime they want," Abby said, "especially at harvest time. However, we're not talking about chores today. We're talking about sewing. I'm wondering how many of you know how to sew a button on the right way."

The teens exchanged puzzled glances and Mikayla said, "I didn't know there was a right or wrong way."

"Then it's time you learned." Abby went to the closest machine and pulled out the chair in front of it. "If each of you will take a seat by a sewing machine, we can get started."

"Us, too?" The boys looked at each other with expressions that suggested they thought she'd lost her mind.

"Ja." She sat and gestured again at the chairs. "One of these days, you'll move out from under your family's roof, and you'll be on your own. What will you do if you need a button sewn on or a piece of clothing repaired?"

"Get a girlfriend to do it?" asked Jack.

Over enthusiastic boos from the young women, another boy called, "Ask *Mamm* or *Grossmammi*?"

"You shouldn't need to ask someone else," Abby said, waving her arms to get their attention and quiet the hubbub again. She was pleased to hear the two Amish teens jumping into the conversation. Even a week ago, they would have been too shy to speak up.

Isaac would approve of the change in them, too. Once a young man was baptized and became a full-fledged member of the *Leit*, it was important he speak up when his opinion was sought.

When the teens were paying attention again, she repeated, "You shouldn't need to ask someone else. Not if you can handle such a simple task as doing a bit of repair work on your own." She smiled. "It's not as if I'm asking you to learn to make a quilt or embroider a sampler. We're going to focus on basic sewing."

"I don't know..." Jack didn't move as the other boys took a single step toward the tables. They paused, too, looking to him as their leader.

"Jack, I hear you've been helping on some of the power equipment at the work sites."

He grinned with impish delight.

At first, the teens hadn't been allowed to do much beyond running errands for the adult volunteers. The kids had asked over and over to help with the actual building. Glen had relented, insisting they only use hand tools. But, when so many volunteers left and didn't return as jobs demanded their attention, Isaac had taken up the teens' quest. He'd urged Glen to let the project leaders at each of the three house sites teach the older teens how to use the equipment. There had been some pushback, but, as her brother had reminded the project leaders, most of them had begun using power tools when they were the same age as the teens. Making sure none of the youngsters ever worked without supervision, they'd begun to make the change a few days ago.

"Big boy toys," Jack said as his smile broadened.

"Big boy *and* big girl toys." Cindi aimed a challenging tilt of her chin at her friend. "I got to use the skip steer yesterday to move some of the trees that had fallen out of the way."

"Just the branches."

"Big branches."

Abby interjected before their teasing became a real argument. "I'm glad you learned to use those machines because that will help you with these."

"My *mamm* uses one of them," Dwight said. "My *grossmammi*, too. They're no big deal."

"No?" Abby crossed her arms in front of herself. "Do you think you'll say the same thing if you end up with that needle in your finger? It won't cut it off as a saw might, but I can guarantee you that it'll get your attention."

That might have been the wrong thing to say because several of the kids stepped away from the machines. With a sigh, she made a quick change in her plans. Deciding to start with a simple task, she urged the kids to sit.

As she began to outline what she wanted them to do and how, she felt contentment for the first time in longer than she could remember. She was supposed to be in Evergreen Corners now. She was certain of that. What she wasn't certain of was how long she could—or should—remain.

David kneaded his lower back with his knuckles as he got out of his truck in front of the community center. Fixing the pump in Ricky Herndon's dairy barn had taken him a lot longer than he'd expected. At one point, he'd been ready to tell Ricky that patching together the system would be a waste of David's time and Ricky's money. The system, which pumped milk from the milkers to the holding tank, wasn't an antique, but was older than David.

He straightened and stretched as he noticed the sun hadn't disappeared over the mountains. A couple of weeks ago, it would have vanished by this hour of the day. That was a welcome sign that spring was on its way to stay.

Not that it felt that way now. Once the sun

was down, the chill would become cold, and he hoped nobody had been foolish enough to believe a couple of warm days in a row meant fragile plants should be put out in the garden.

He opened the door to the community center, entered and halted in midstep. He wanted to rub his eyes to make sure he was seeing what he thought he was. The youth group was sitting around tables, like a quilting circle, each of them with a needle and thread they were using with such concentration they didn't look up to see who'd come in. They were chatting and checking each other's work.

In the kitchen, Abby was busy with three other women. She must not have heard the door because she was talking with a short woman he didn't know, her back to him.

He went to where Mikayla sat at a table with the other girls. They each held a needle and were darting it in and out of shirts, sewing on buttons.

"Hey, Mr. Riehl," said Lily as she raised her head. At her voice, the other girls looked up.

"What are you up to?" he asked, though it was obvious. Each of the teens was doing the same task.

"Before she went to the hospital," Mikayla answered, "Mrs. Blomgren planned to teach us some basic sewing. Abby decided we should learn now and surprise her."

He hadn't been sure she'd acknowledge him after the sharp words they'd had at breakfast that morning. She'd insisted she would ride her bike to school and refused to give any credence to his argument she was making herself an easy target for the bullies. She'd ridden away without heeding a word he'd said.

"We're doing some on the machines," Lily said when he remained silent, "and the rest by hand."

Cindi laughed as she nudged Mikayla with an elbow. "We're crushing it while the boys haven't gotten one right yet."

"We're taking our time," shot back Jack. "We're going to be experts at sewing on buttons so we won't need you silly girls any longer."

Lily leaned toward him. "You've got to leave more space beneath the button to wind the thread around the base so it can be tilted in and out of the buttonhole. Do it like Abby showed us."

David left the kids debating the proper way to sew on the buttons and walked to the kitchen pass-through window. He rested his arms on the counter while he waited for Abby to have a moment to talk to him.

It didn't take long. One of the women elbowed

her and motioned with her head toward where he was standing.

When Abby turned, his breath caught. It'd been a couple of days since he'd held her at Doris's house, but his longing to draw her into his arms again hadn't diminished. That one stolen second had filled his thoughts during the day and delighted his dreams at night.

"Hi!" she called as she walked into the main room. "I didn't expect to see you now that Mikayla is riding her bike home."

"I wanted to stop by to ask you if you'd had a chance to check on Doris." He didn't want to go into the details of the disagreement he and Mikayla had gotten into that morning. Knowing Abby would have suggestions on how to bridge the chasm between them, he said nothing. This was something *he* had to fix, not Abby. "How's Doris doing?"

"Well. When I visited, her great-niece told me Doris has been listening to the instructions her *doktor* gave her. So far, at least."

"I'm glad to hear that. I'd planned on stopping over this afternoon, but today's project took a lot longer than I'd expected."

"Would you like a cup of *kaffi*?"

"Do you have some fresh?"

"Always." She laughed as she went to where the pot was on the other side of the pass-through. With ease, she stayed out of the other volunteers' way. "People are constantly in and out of here, and most of them want something warm to drink after working outside."

"It's rumored that spring is supposed to arrive one of these days."

"When it does, we'll put the *kaffi* over ice cubes."

While Abby prepared a large cup for him, he watched Mikayla with the other teens. She seemed much more at ease with them than she had a month ago. Instead of staying by herself off to the side, she sat among them and laughed as Cindi tried to help Reece thread a needle. When she said something that made the teens roar with laughter, he couldn't keep from smiling.

"She's doing better every day," he said as Abby handed him the cup and gestured to the back door. He followed her, knowing that she had something on her mind she didn't want to discuss in front of the others. Doris? Mikayla? Something or someone else?

When Abby sat on a winter-battered bench in the tangle of weeds that was supposed to be a garden, he sat beside her. He waited for her to say whatever was on her mind.

"Mikayla is doing better every day," she said in a somber tone, "but prepare yourself that she'll have bad days as well as *gut* ones.

Grief wants to cling to us for as long as it can torment us."

"'And God shall wipe away all tears from their eyes,'" he whispered.

"That's from Revelation."

He faced her. "I know. Someone shared it with me at Boyd's funeral, and I have thought of it often since while listening to Mikayla crying in her room. I wonder why God hasn't wiped the tears from her eyes as He promised."

"You must have faith that a day will come when the tears stop. A heart doesn't heal quickly, even with God's help. It's the price we pay for the ability He gave us to love. With that gift comes the cost of losing someone we love."

"Have you lost someone?"

"*Ja*. My *mamm*, I mean—"

"Your mother. I've heard that word before." He shifted so he could see her face. "I don't think I've ever heard anyone mention that your mother died. I'm sorry about that."

"*Danki*. She died when I was little more than a *boppli*."

"Is your father alive?"

"He is, and he remarried a *wunderbaar* woman who makes him happy after many years of him struggling with depression. I tell God *danki* every morning and night in my prayers for bringing her into our lives." She put her hand over his, startling him. "Have faith, David. God brought healing to my family when I thought nothing ever would make us happy again. He'll do the same for Mikayla. And for you, because I know you have lost a dear friend."

"My best friend. Boyd and I were friends from the minute we met our first day of school. When we weren't in the same class, we spent every possible second together on the playground or after school. We worked together in our first jobs, and we saved our money and bought our first cars within days of each other. Almost every milestone in the life of a boy and a young man I shared with him, including falling in love. That's where our paths diverged. Chelsea, the girl I thought would be with me forever, dumped me the same night Boyd proposed to Jill, Mikayla's mother."

"Ouch."

"Yeah, ouch. Being happy for Boyd and Jill meant I couldn't waste time feeling sorry for myself."

"Don't you see, David? That's what Mikayla needs. A reason for the two of you to be happy so she isn't imprisoned by her grief. You had your friend and his future wife to help you through the toughest time you'd ever faced. You need to help her."

"I would if I knew how."

"You know how, David. Stop feeling guilty for every little thing that happens. Give that guilt and your pain to God. He's strong enough to shoulder the burden and let you find joy again."

"You make it sound both easy and as if it's a sure thing."

"Isn't it? One of my *grossmammi*'s favorite verses was from Romans. Romans 15, verse 13 to be exact. 'Now the God of hope fill you with all joy and peace in believing, that ye may abound in hope, through the power of the Holy Ghost.' Joy and peace and hope. What *wunderbaar* gifts from God!" She smiled at him. "All you have to do is open your heart to accept them."

He started to reply, but a woman appeared in the doorway and called to Abby in a rather frantic tone. Smoke billowed out the door around her.

Jumping to her feet, Abby ran into the kitchen. He stood to follow, then paused when he heard someone call, "It's out!"

He saw that was true, so he headed toward the street before Abby could return. Their conversation had been wandering into areas of his life he wanted to keep off-limits, even from himself. And if he knew what was good for him and for Abby, he wouldn't let her entice him to go there again.

Not ever.

Chapter Twelve

David decided the mid-April morning was just what the day before Easter should be. Frost clinging to the grass would soon vanish. Bright sunshine poured into the bathroom as he finished shaving. Washing the last of the soap off his chin, he hurried downstairs.

The newspaper was waiting by the porch and he hurried to bring it inside when the cold morning air sliced through his clothes. He made breakfast and waited for Mikayla to come downstairs. During the week, she waited until the last possible minute so she could grab a couple of pieces of toast and a banana, then run out the door to get her bike and head to school without a word spoken to him. The weekends were different. She didn't have the late bell at school as an excuse to avoid spending time with him.

As Abby was?

The thought seemed petty, but he hadn't had a chance to speak with Abby since their conversation behind the community center two days ago. He'd thought he might run into her at Doris's house. Going there twice in the past week, he'd been told that he'd "just missed her" each time. He got the same response when he went to fix a door that wouldn't close properly at the Mennonite chapel. Abby had been working in the kitchen until minutes before he'd shown up.

It would be easy to accuse her of avoiding him. However, he knew that wasn't the case.

"It's got to be coincidental," he said to himself.

"What?" asked Mikayla as she came into the kitchen. She was wearing an old T-shirt and a bathrobe. Though she'd braided her hair, strands had come loose while she'd slept.

"Talking to myself." He put scrambled eggs and bacon on two plates and carried them to the table.

She poured orange juice while he made toast. It was a choreographed performance they'd perfected in the past ten months. The tasks kept them occupied so they didn't have to talk, and they never bumped into each other as they crisscrossed the kitchen.

They sat at the same time, and Mikayla bowed her head over her clasped hands while he said grace. As soon as he was finished, she picked up one section of the newspaper he'd tossed on the table and raised it between them. She might as well have put out a sign that said No Trespassing.

David ate his breakfast in silence. He considered reading another section of the paper, but that didn't appeal to him. When Mikayla had first moved in the day after the car accident, he'd tried to engage her in conversation during breakfast. He'd come to realize it might be a lost cause, but he couldn't give up. She'd lost so much, and she shouldn't be suffering alone.

She's not alone. She has her friends. She has Abby. The voice in his mind refused to be quiescent. Arguing with it would be futile, but how much longer did he need to wait for Mikayla to stop acting as if his house were a temporary home?

Not having an answer to that question—and to so many others, he said, "By the way, Pastor Hershey was hoping you'd help today."

There was a long pause and he wished he could see her expression on the other side of the newspaper. Was she rolling her eyes as she did so often when he made a comment? Or maybe she was listening.

"I know," she said, getting up and putting her dishes in the dishwasher. "I told him I'd be glad to help."

"With what?"

She stared at him as if he'd sprouted an antenna in the middle of his forehead. "The Easter egg hunt." She startled him by grinning. "Didn't you see the flyer at the community center?"

He didn't want to say that when he went in the community center, he usually had eyes only for Abby. "I guess I missed it."

"The flyer is bright lime green and in almost every window in town."

"Maybe I need to borrow your glasses."

That earned him a rare smile. "I should get dressed. I don't want to be late."

"When does it start?"

"Around 11:00 a.m." She went upstairs.

He folded his hands together on the table and bent his head once more. "God, thank You for convincing her to open up to me. Reach into her heart and ease its pain. Give her hope, like it says in that verse Abby's grandmother loved. Hope and joy."

A half hour later, David heard Mikayla come down the stairs. He pulled on a light coat as he crossed the kitchen and met Mikayla by the door.

She'd rebraided her hair and twisted it behind her head, looking less like a child and more like a young woman. She wore a pale blue coat that reached almost to her knees. When he noticed how short the sleeves were, he made a mental note to talk to her later about getting a new spring coat. She hadn't mentioned anything about clothes in the time she'd been living with him. He'd thought teenage girls loved clothes, but Mikayla seemed to have no interest in them, though he'd seen her at the grocery store paging through teen fashion magazines a couple of times when she hadn't realized he was paying attention.

If she hadn't moved into his house before the flood, she'd have nothing. He'd never forget her blank countenance when they'd gone to see what was left of the house where she'd grown up. There hadn't been more than a crumbling chimney and a few broken boards. Everything else had been swept away.

"I should have said this before. Happy Easter eve," he said with a smile as he held the door for her.

"Happy Easter eve." She didn't meet his eyes, but a hint of a smile pulled at her lips. When she climbed on her bike, she waved before pedaling toward the center of the village.

By the time David reached the village green, families were already gathering. The Easter egg hunt was sponsored by the churches and several merchants in town. Mikayla stood with her friends, who'd gathered beside the bandstand that had been battered by the floodwaters.

Teens needed to be independent. He'd felt that way when he was younger, too. Yet he kept wishing some part of Mikayla could be a little bit dependent on him. Something to show him she considered him a part of her life.

When he saw Abby carrying a large punch bowl filled with pink liquid topped with a chunk of sherbet, he rushed to her. He did a slalom through the plastic eggs that had been tossed into the grass for the children to collect. He took the bowl and followed her to a table where cups and napkins were already waiting.

"Danki," she said with a smile. "Isn't it a *wunderbaar* day for little ones?"

He couldn't pull his gaze from her pretty face to look at the children, who were eager for the fun to start. "I didn't expect to see you here today."

"Why not? We volunteers are a part of the community while we're here, and we want to help keep Evergreen Corners's traditions alive after the flood."

"No, it's not that. I didn't realize Amish hunted for Easter eggs."

"Our *kinder* love coloring eggs as much as *Englisch kinder* do." Her smile wavered. "You have some odd notions of us. We're people like everyone else."

Except your people chased my family away because of... His thought halted as he wondered anew why his parents hadn't shared why they'd left their Amish community. The plain volunteers he'd met in Evergreen Corners, even Abby's exacting brother, were warmhearted. Were they the best of their kind or were they a true example? If they were...

He stopped that thought. Going around and around when he didn't have enough information was silly. He needed to talk with his parents and get the truth.

"Anything else I can help with?" he asked.

"Later you can help toss out more eggs for the next group to gather. For now, I've got everything covered."

He was sure she did. In that way, she was a lot like her older brother. They both liked to have details tended to before any new project began.

David let out an exultant yell along with the other adults as the youngest children rushed forward to collect eggs. Several of the little ones had been dressed as bunnies and their ears bobbed with their uneven steps. Parents were allowed to help the preschoolers, and he wasn't surprised when Abby offered a hand to a mother who had three little ones who might have been triplets.

He watched as she bent to show a toddler how to pick up the plastic eggs and the chocolate eggs without squashing them between his fingers. The harried mother, who was overseeing her other youngsters, flashed her a grateful smile.

"David, come and help," she called.

For a moment, he hesitated. Most of the fathers were lingering on the sidelines, some keeping their older children from rushing onto the field to grab the eggs. Others were talking together and not watching the scramble on the field. A few, however, were squatting beside their little ones, urging them to pay attention to the candy instead of a bird or a twig or a bug.

He wondered which sort of father he would have been if Mikayla had been as young as these toddlers when she'd come to live with him. Maybe it was time he found out. With a widening grin, he joined the hunt and soon found himself laughing along with Abby and the children. He looked toward the bandstand and saw Mikayla laughing. When his daughter gave him a thumbs-up, he wanted to dance in the middle of the green.

He glanced at Abby. Had she seen Mikayla's reaction? When she smiled, he knew she hadn't missed it. A sense of something he could only describe as joy filled him, astonishing him because he couldn't remember the last time he'd felt this way. He knew he wanted to savor it now and feel it again.

Soon.

What a *wunderbaar* service it had been! To celebrate the Resurrection with friends who'd become as close as family filled Abby's heart with happiness. Everyone had sounded exultant while singing the familiar hymns, and the *kinder* had been less antsy as they'd listened to the message of hope and love and promise. It had been a true coming together of a community of faith on a wondrous day.

As she cleaned the tables after the men had finished their midday meal, which was served outside on the lawn behind the chapel, she chatted with the women who were bringing food from the kitchen for themselves and the *kinder*. She paused when she saw two familiar forms, one of them pushing a bicycle, walking toward them.

Abby wiped her hands on her apron as she went to greet Mikayla and Reece. The two teenagers looked uneasy when they paused by the kitchen door.

"Happy *Oschderdaag*!" she said and then added, "Happy Easter day!"

Mikayla leaned her bike against a tree. "I hope we're not intruding."

"How could you be intruding? Today we're all family celebrating a glorious day." She looped her arm through Mikayla's and led the girl to the table where the women and *kinder* were beginning the communal meal. "Are you hungry? Would you like a sandwich?"

Reece gazed at the thick ham and turkey sandwiches with obvious yearning, but Mikayla replied, "It's your Easter dinner, not ours."

"Nonsense," said Rachel Yoder as she patted the end of the bench where she and her young daughters sat. "We love to share."

Abby grinned. "And, besides, you don't want these sandwiches to go to waste, ain't so?"

The teens didn't need another invitation. They joined the meal and the conversation that switched from *Deitsch* for their benefit. Mikayla updated Abby on Doris's recovery, because Mikayla and Reece had stopped by the old woman's house.

"So you made your special egg this year for Doris?" Abby hid her sorrow that the girl hadn't given it to David as she used to share it with her *daed*.

"No, I didn't make her an egg." Mikayla took

a big bite of her sandwich. "She said she hopes we come to visit soon."

"That old machine of hers isn't that different," Reece added, "than the ones you taught us to use."

Rachel glanced at Abby in a silent question. Abby told her new friend about the teen group and the sewing lessons. When Mikayla and Reece asked the little ones about the egg hunt the previous day, they heard plenty of stories about the treasures in the plastic eggs. Tiny books, rings and more chocolate had been hidden in them by the donors.

After the meal, Reece and Mikayla joined the softball game played in a field that was part of a now-abandoned farm. Abby went inside to help with the cleaning up. She paused when David walked into the community center.

"I've been expecting you," she said as she met him by the door. "I'm assuming you're looking for Mikayla."

"She said she was going for a ride after church, and I thought she'd be home by now."

"She and Reece came to share our Sunday meal. They're playing ball now."

He relaxed. "I should have known she'd end up here."

"Here? Why?"

"Because you're here." He gave her a sad

smile as they walked outdoors so he could see his daughter playing with the others. "I've learned that whenever we lock horns, Mikayla will find a way to be with you."

"If *daed* says no, then maybe *mamm*…"

"No, she doesn't think of you as her mother. She sees you as the big sister she wishes she had." He ground the tip of his boot into the muddy ground.

"What she wants is what you're offering her. Somehow, she needs to come to see that."

"I agree, but how?"

"Talk to her."

He gave a mirthless laugh while they continued walking past the chapel and the impromptu ball field and toward a scraggly orchard. "I've talked to her until I'm blue in the face. I ask her opinions. I talk about her friends and what they're doing. I ask her about the latest book the kids are reading or the show they're watching. Yet, most of the time, I feel as if I'm talking to empty air. I can see her. I can hear her, but it's like she's not there."

"Is it different when you're with the teen group?"

"Not much. Most of the time, she uses her friends as a buffer. I think she encourages them to talk to me so she can avoid doing so."

Abby shook her head, not reaching out to him

as she wanted to. They were out of sight and out of earshot from the ball players, so she resisted touching him, unsure if she could let him go if she did. "You're wrong, David. I've never seen her do or say anything to them to urge them to talk to you."

"They do, and she doesn't."

She stopped and leaned against the prickly bark of a twisted apple tree's trunk. "They talk to you because they want to, not because she persuades them to."

"That doesn't make sense."

"Why not? Don't lots of people talk to you?"

A smile slid across his face as he reached up and picked a shriveled apple off a branch over her head. In a few weeks, the trees would become white clouds of apple blossoms. "Some of them talk to me far too much."

"That's because they like you."

"I don't know about that."

She frowned at him. "We Amish consider *hochmut*—pride—a sin, but I think false modesty is as much of one. I'm going to be blunt. People talk to you because they like you. I've seen it over and over."

"So Mikayla doesn't like me. Is that what you're saying?"

"David Riehl! If you want a pity party, find someone else to have it with." When he laughed, she looked at him in amazement. "Did I say something wrong?"

"No, you said the right thing. Pity party. I never expected to hear those words come out of the mouth of an Amish woman."

"I've learned a lot from the kids." She laughed. "And I'm not the only one. I've heard Isaac say phrases he's never used before. Not that I'd ever point that out to him because he'd be horrified."

"If you ever decide to do so, let me know. I'd like to see his reaction."

Her laugh became a giggle. "And I thought you believed you weren't any fun, David."

"I'm not, but—"

"You *are* fun, and you are funny, and who-ever said otherwise was wrong."

"You believe that?" His voice deepened as he moved a half step toward her.

"Ja." She gazed into his eyes and saw a storm of powerful emotions in them.

When he edged an inch closer to her, his hands rose to take her face between them. He leaned forward to brush her lips with his own.

She raised her hands to push him away, as she should, but his silent persuasion urged her instead to wrap her arms around his shoulders. Delight filled her and exploded as if she were a firework decorating the sky.

Then he raised his mouth away. She murmured a protest but halted herself when she heard the despair in his voice as he said, "Abby... Abby, I'm so—"

"Please," she whispered. "Please don't say you're sorry."

"But I am. Because you are what you are and I'm what I am, I'm sorry I'll never be able to kiss you like this ever again." He clasped her face again and pressed his lips to hers.

He released her so quickly she rocked on her heels. As she gripped the tree behind her, he strode away. Her tears blurred his form as she fought not to give chase.

She'd promised herself and God that she wouldn't make the same mistake again. She wouldn't follow her foolish heart because nothing *gut* ever came of it.

Yet she'd heeded her heart when she'd surrendered to her yearning for his kiss.

And she might have ruined the best friendship she'd ever had.

Chapter Thirteen

What was the name of that old song? "What a Difference a Day Makes"? That was the one, and David wondered if he'd ever been aware of the truth in those few words than he was on during the week after Easter. As he drove south from Ludlow, almost an hour to the north of Evergreen Corners, he wished he could start the day over again.

Not just today, but yesterday and the day before that, too.

"Would it make any difference?" he asked himself as he slowed for a stop sign, eager to get home.

Watching the traffic rush past in both directions while he waited for a chance to turn left, he wished today hadn't been the day he'd agreed to work on the refrigerator at Moo Beans, a coffee shop near the road leading up to the ski resort on Okemo Mountain. He usually didn't travel so far for work, but he'd done other jobs for the owner since the original Moo Beans opened in Evergreen Corners four years ago.

Back before Mikayla became his responsibility. Back before he had to guard every word he said and everything he did in an effort to prevent another quarrel with his daughter. Today's had been because Mikayla didn't want to wear her boots to school. It was the same one they'd had most days since the snow had begun to melt and she'd started riding her bike.

Today, it'd been a battle he'd conceded for two reasons. He'd realized if he persisted in insisting she wear her boots to school and carry her sneakers in her backpack, she would have changed from boots to shoes as soon as she was out of his sight. He didn't want her to feel she had to sneak around, because that would drive them apart rather than open doors for communication.

Now he sounded like Glen, who was always talking about ways to keep ideas flowing among the volunteers.

However, the real reason he'd given in was that Mikayla had spent a good part of the previous evening in her room, upset and crying. Not that she'd shared the reason for her tears with him. He'd asked, and she'd made it clear she didn't want his help.

He could imagine what Abby would say. She would tell him…

Dismay stabbed him. Would she speak to him after he'd kissed her on Easter?

He refused to think of that, but he was no more successful than he'd been for the past forty-eight hours. He'd made a big mistake. Hadn't his parents spent almost of his whole life warning him not to get mixed up with the Amish? If he'd listened, he wouldn't be drowning in guilt because he'd hurt Abby and destroyed any chance of having her help with Mikayla.

David frowned as he pulled into his driveway and saw an unfamiliar car parked by the house. Whose was it? The silver car had Massachusetts plates. Maybe some tourist had gotten lost and decided to turn around in his driveway.

The car was empty. Why would somebody from Massachusetts leave their car in his driveway?

As he opened his truck door, he wondered if the car had broken down. That made no sense. Everyone had a cell phone and, if the driver had called for a repair truck or a tow, wouldn't he or she be waiting by the car?

"There he is!" came a familiar voice from the porch.

David was astonished to see his parents, Ed and Nora Riehl, sitting in rocking chairs he needed to paint. As he approached, they stood. His mother waved as if he were on a ship sailing off into the ocean.

Why hadn't they told him they were visiting?

"David, it's so good to see you!" Mother rushed to enfold him in a hug, but he held up a quick hand to halt her before the dirt on his work clothes got on her pretty navy blue suit. She contented herself with giving him a quick kiss on the cheek.

He saw her faint frown and recalled he'd forgotten to shave that morning after the argument with Mikayla.

His father shook his hand and smiled. "You look surprised. We told you we were coming today."

"No, you didn't. Did you leave a message on my cell or the shop phone?"

"I don't know," his father said with a chuckle. "Ask your mother. She's the one who called."

"I didn't call, Ed." His mother shook her head. "You said you were going to."

"No, Nora, you told me you were going to."

His mother threw her hands up in the air, the charms on her bangles chiming against one another. "Oh, well. I guess we should say, 'Surprise, David!' Here we are!"

Looking at his soiled clothes, he said, "Let me change, and we'll chat."

"Sounds good," Father replied.

David was startled to realize that his father's *good* sounded close to Abby's *gut*. Odd, how he'd never stopped to think the faint accent on their words had come from their plain upbringing. When he was growing up, they'd simply sounded to him like his parents. Now, after spending time with Abby and the other Amish volunteers, he recognized the accent. He must have spoken the same way once, but somewhere along the way, he'd lost that inflection.

"Where's Mikayla?" His mother glanced at her watch as they climbed the porch stairs. "School can't still be in session, can it? It's after four."

"She's working in the village. She's part of a group of teens who have been assisting in repairing houses and businesses after last fall's flood."

"What about her studies?" Mother sat in a rocker again. "She's not going to get into a good college if she doesn't keep her grades up."

"She's doing well." He didn't add that Mikayla avoided any conversations about her future. Or the past, for that matter. Envy cramped his heart. How wonderful would it have been never to think about the past?

Mikayla *did* think about the past, he knew. She might not speak of it, but her father and the life she'd lost must have been on her mind. He'd learned that from Abby as he'd discovered so many other things about his daughter.

Teenagers are like onions. He wanted to smile each time he recalled Abby's words. So simple and yet true. Every day he was discovering something new about Mikayla. Was he seeing her in a new way or was she revealing more about the girl he'd thought he'd known but hadn't?

He'd been learning more about Abby each day, too, until he'd messed up everything by kissing her. His practiced distrust of anything Amish had disappeared. At least as far as she was concerned. He reserved judgment about the sect as a whole.

Or, more specifically, her brother Isaac, who hadn't relented in his determination to keep Abby from spending any more time than necessary with an *Englischer*.

He had to admit her brother had been right.

Abby wiped the sheen of sweat from her forehead. As the weather continued to warm, they were going to have to figure out something to do to vent the built-up heat in the community center kitchen. Her hope that there were screens for the windows stored somewhere else in the building had come to naught.

Rachel opened the door and wafted her hands to try to keep out the bugs attracted by the aromas from the ovens. "We need to do something about this."

"I know. I was thinking the same."

"We need a screen door," said another volunteer. "Why don't you ask David, Abby? He'd be willing to do that."

She forced herself not to flinch at the mention of David's name. Nobody else knew what had happened in the orchard, and she must keep it that way. If Isaac learned that David had kissed her, her brother would ship her home immediately and insist she not return.

"There's no sense bothering David when we don't have a door," she said.

"He might know where to find one that will fit. You know him best, so do you mind checking with him?"

As every face in the kitchen turned toward her, Abby reminded herself of the promise she'd made to God. She'd do what she could to help and stop listening to her heart.

She ignored her instincts that warned her not to go to David's house. If he wasn't there—

and she wasn't sure if she wanted him to be or not—she'd leave him a message about putting a screen door on the kitchen. If she didn't speak to him today, she would have to eventually. She suspected delaying would make that encounter more difficult.

When she walked up the driveway ten minutes later, she was surprised to see strangers sitting with David on the porch. The man and the woman must be related to him because she saw something of each of them in his face. However, they couldn't be more unlike him in how they dressed. She'd never seen him in anything more formal than khakis and a neatly pressed shirt. Most of the time he seemed to prefer jeans and a casual polo shirt or T-shirt.

The man with his neat mustache and dark plastic-rimmed glasses wore a navy jacket over matching trousers. A pale blue tie clipped with a gold clasp accented his pristine white shirt and the handkerchief in his pocket. His shoes shone like sunlight on the brook.

Beside him, the woman was dressed as formally. Her navy suit, made of a fabric Abby guessed might be silk because of its sheen, emphasized her figure. Her eyes were a similar color, astonishing Abby because she'd never seen eyes of such a hue. Jewelry—necklaces, earrings and bracelets—glittered with each motion she made. She appeared as tall as her husband, but then Abby noticed she was wearing shoes with ultrahigh, pencil-thin heels.

The newcomers stared at her and Abby realized they expected her to speak first. She wasn't sure what to say. Searching her mind for something that wouldn't sound forced, she decided on the obvious.

"I didn't realize you had company, David." She glanced at the silver car parked next to his truck. "I should have. *Es dutt mir leed.*" She flinched when her self-consciousness led her to speak *Deitsch* again. "Oops. I meant to say 'I'm sorry.' I didn't intend to interrupt you and your guests."

David's voice was emotionless as he came down the steps and motioned for her to join the others. "Come and meet my parents."

She smiled, but her expression wavered when neither of the newcomers did. In fact, they regarded her with cool, suspicious expressions that reminded her of David's the first time she'd met him when he'd come to fix the freezer. She hadn't understood his antipathy then and she didn't understand his parents' now.

Both Ed and Nora Riehl gave her the faintest of nods while David spoke their names and introduced her. Reminding herself that *Englisch-*

ers often felt uncomfortable with plain folk, she made sure her smile was in place again.

"It's nice to meet you," she said. It wasn't a lie. She *wanted* it to be a nice moment, but she hadn't known his parents would look and act as these people did.

How could she have known anything about them? David seldom spoke about his family other than Mikayla. He and Abby had talked about so many other things, but she was startled to discover she didn't know if he had brothers or sisters. He'd never mentioned either.

"We didn't know there were any Amish in Evergreen Corners, did we, Ed?" asked Mrs. Riehl.

"Never heard of any around here. There weren't any during the years we lived here." He looked down his nose at her as if she were a germ about to infect the perfection of the place.

"We're here to help with rebuilding Evergreen Corners after the flood." She kept her voice light, but was careful not to add that one Amish family had already decided to remain in the small town and was hoping others would stay, too.

As she wished she could. *Stop listening to your stupid heart!*

"We didn't realize that," Mr. Riehl said.

"David didn't mention anything to us, did he, Nora?"

"Nothing at all."

Abby waited for David to respond. When he remained silent, she said, "Amish Helping Hands is the name of the organization that oversees our volunteers." She tried to smile but halted when she realized she must look like she was grimacing. "We've been working with the Mennonite Disaster Service and other plain groups to help local merchants get their businesses going and to build homes for families who lost everything. If you have some free time while you're visiting, you should pay a visit to the homes that have replaced those washed away."

"We might," Mrs. Riehl said in a tone that made it clear she had no plans to do so.

Growing more desperate to put an end to the uncomfortable conversation, Abby said, "David, I came over to talk to you about getting a screen door for the community center kitchen. I can come back later."

"No, you don't need to do that." He turned to his parents. "If you want to get unpacked, I'll get supper started after I'm done with Abby." Some emotion flickered through his eyes. Regret at his choice of words? Or relief he'd announced to her—and to his parents—he didn't intend to spend more time with her than necessary?

His parents exchanged a worried glance but complied. As soon as the door closed behind them, David took Abby by the arm and steered her to the far side of the truck.

"My mother is an eavesdropper," he said without apology as he moved his hand away.

"I don't know what you're worried about. I gave you my message and I should get back to—"

"Abby, do you know what's bothering Mikayla? She came home a half hour ago, and she barely greeted my parents before heading upstairs."

She closed her eyes. "She came to talk to me this morning before school. She had a run-in with Hunter and his band of hooligans again last night at the wrestling match at school."

"Is that what it was?" He shook his head and sighed. "She wouldn't talk about it last night, and I heard her crying when I went to bed. I knocked on her door. She told me she was fine, that she was reading something sad."

"You didn't believe her?"

"You don't have to make it a question. No, I didn't believe her. She might have been reading something sad, but I didn't—not for an instant—believe she was fine."

"You've got to get her to talk to you."

"I know, but how?"

"I don't know. We both need to pray for an answer." She laced her fingers together behind her, so they wouldn't reach out to console him. If she touched him when her feelings were so raw, so new, so tender, she wasn't sure what might happen next. She almost laughed at the thought. She knew *exactly* what would happen and she knew what the consequences would be. "I should get back to the kitchen."

He stepped around her to keep her from walking away. "Abby, I'm sorry…"

"No, please. I asked you not to say it on Sunday." She didn't want to tell him that her heart would break and might never be repaired if she heard him say he regretted sharing her first kiss.

He nodded. "I won't say I'm sorry about that, but I've got to say I'm sorry for my parents' behavior."

Glad he'd changed the subject away from the precious kiss whose memory she knew she'd treasure for as long as she lived, she asked, "Did I do or say something wrong? I didn't mean to offend them."

"You didn't."

"Are you certain?"

He looked at the door where his parents had gone inside. When she followed his gaze, she saw the curtains on a nearby window being flicked aside. "I'm certain. Sometimes... Well, they're tired from their flight and the drive from Boston."

She wondered what he'd been going to say before he'd interrupted himself. Sometimes his parents did or said what? She couldn't quiz him because she could tell he was upset and she didn't want to add to it. So she thanked him for agreeing to help and left.

As she walked toward the village green, the truth dogged her heels. Something was wrong at the Riehl house. Something was wrong beyond Mikayla being bullied and David struggling to be the *daed* she needed.

Something was wrong, and she had to figure out what it was if she had any chance of helping him.

Standing in his kitchen after supper, David watched their car's lights vanish into the darkness. His parents hadn't been happy about being "tricked" into talking with an Amish woman. His apology, which he hoped would soothe their ruffled feathers, had been as useless. He wondered if they'd return. He could recall wondering the same thing often during his childhood when they'd left on yet another trip without him. He'd known they loved him, and they made sure he was provided for, but he could see—looking back—he was never sure if they were happier when he wasn't around.

He didn't move until he heard light footsteps on the stairs. He looked over his shoulder and saw Mikayla heading for the refrigerator.

"Your parents giving you a hard time?" she asked as she took out a bottle of juice.

He was about to tell her how shortsighted and mistaken his parents were. He was ready to spout off how annoyed he was at them. Every word vanished when the girl turned to face him. How could he complain about his parents when she'd lost both of hers? He was certain that, no matter how upset she'd been with Boyd and how often, she would have forgiven him. He had the chance to make things better. She didn't.

"No more of a hard time than I've given you," he replied, keeping his voice light.

She rolled her eyes before surprising him by leaning against the counter instead of sprinting back up the stairs. She took a deep drink, wiped her mouth with her hand and asked, "So what are you going to do now?"

"Go to bed. There's not anything else I can do," he said, knowing he had to be honest with her—and himself—now. "They said not to wait up."

"They ignored your apology."

He hadn't guessed she'd hear his parents' voices up in her room. "They're angry."

"Then they should have stayed and talked it out. That's what Dad said was the right thing to do."

He fought not to let his gasp escape. It was the first time Mikayla had mentioned Boyd to him in casual conversation since his best friend's death. "Your dad was right."

"He was, and I think not talking things out when you can is wrong. You never know if you'll have another chance." She tilted the bottle again then walked toward the stairs.

"Mikayla?"

She looked over her shoulder but didn't reply.

"You're a pretty smart kid, you know that?"

"Yep."

"I appreciate you giving me your opinion. I appreciate it a lot."

"She said you would." She hurried up the stairs.

She? He didn't need to ask to whom Mikayla was referring. His daughter didn't listen to many people, but she did take Abby's advice to heart.

His shoulders stiffened as he realized he wasn't the only one Abby was trying to fix. He forced them to ease from their taut stance. How could he be irked with Abby when she'd found a way to reach Mikayla after he'd failed miserably?

Everything came back to Abby.

He sat at the kitchen table. Leaning his head forward to rest on his folded hands, he prayed as he hadn't in longer than he could remember. "Dear Lord, help me know what to do now."

Chapter Fourteen

Stop beating yourself up about David's parents.
The thought replayed endlessly in Abby's head as she got up, said her morning prayers, dressed and went to the community center. It echoed beneath the clatter of pots and griddles as she worked with other volunteers to make breakfast. When she spoke with the men and women who would be braving the afternoon's spring showers to start another house, the words in her mind repeated as an undercurrent almost as vicious as the flood that had torn through the town.

What had she done to upset them? David had assured her that she hadn't said anything wrong, but his dismay had been displayed on his face. He'd been as tense as the teen volunteers were when they thought Hunter Keyes and his band of bullies were nearby.

She shrugged aside that thought. She shouldn't be comparing Mr. and Mrs. Riehl to teenage troublemakers. They'd raised a *gut* son, and they hadn't been unkind to her. Just cold enough to give her frostbite.

Because they don't like the Amish.

The thought made her stop as she was about to take her favorite mixing bowl out of the cupboard. Where had that idea come from? Now that it had erupted into her mind, she couldn't ignore it.

"Excuse me," murmured one of the other volunteers who needed to get to the cupboard.

Abby moved aside, not noticing who it was. She was too mired in her conflicting thoughts. She didn't want to believe the Riehls had such negative feelings about the Amish.

Or that David had.

Was prejudice the reason he had acted so oddly the first time they'd met? She pressed her hand over her aching heart. How could it want to belong to a man who'd been raised to dislike the Amish?

No, she couldn't be certain that was the case. After all, why would his parents have such a prejudice against plain folks? It didn't make any sense. Most *Englischers*, if they thought about the Amish, found them pleasantly quaint. She'd heard an *Englisch* tourist in Bird-in-Hand use those exact words.

Pleasantly quaint.

"Abby?" asked Rachel with an urgency that suggested she'd tried to reach past Abby's reverie more than once.

"Sorry. Lost in thought."

"I've got a question nobody else seems to know the answer to. How do you deal with food allergies?"

"We try to have a variety of dishes, but we do ask people when they arrive if they've got allergies or sensitivities." She smiled. "Didn't someone ask you?"

"*Ja*, and I was asked if Loribeth and Eva do." She smiled as she spoke her toddler daughters' names.

"Do they?"

"Not so far, I'm grateful to God. I've seen what families have endured when someone can't eat the food everyone else can. It's like having to run a restaurant."

Abby laughed. "Like we do here. We provide food for vegetarians and for those with salt issues and various allergies. I wish I had more recipes for those who have a problem with gluten."

"I've got a few if you'd like them," Rachel offered.

"I'd love them. Does someone in your family or among your *Leit* need to have gluten-free dishes?"

"They're just recipes I've picked up through the years." She turned away to put the plates on top of the others in the cupboards. "This isn't the first time I've volunteered for a mobilization like this."

"You must have been talking with Glen. He likes to use words like *mobilization* when he talks about his volunteer projects."

Rachel picked up a big pan from the dishwasher and opened cupboard doors, looking for where it belonged. When Abby directed her to the pantry, she said, *"Danki."*

Abby reached for a dishcloth to wipe down a counter, then halted when Glen entered. He looked around the main room, then came toward the kitchen. When she called a *gute mariye*, he smiled.

"Have you seen David Riehl?" he asked.

"No. He hasn't been here."

"Okay, I took a chance. I'll call him at home later." He turned toward the door, then paused. "If you see him, have him give me a call or drop by my office."

"I will." She wanted to ask why Glen was looking for David, but kept her lips buttoned.

As if she'd called the question after him, Glen

faced her. "I need to talk to him right away. We have to decide which families will be getting the next houses rebuilt, and the St. Pierre house came up on our list. I need to know if he wants us to move forward with it now or not."

"St. Pierre house?" She couldn't believe the words as she spoke them. "Are you talking about Mikayla's *daed*'s house?"

"Mikayla's house now."

"It was destroyed in the flood?"

He nodded. "It was set below the covered bridge and dam. When the dam failed, the water destroyed two houses in the curve of the brook. Washed them away as if they'd never been there."

"I didn't know. Nobody ever mentioned it."

"Hmm… I thought I did the day I asked you and David to take over the teen program." His smile returned. "By the way, I'm hearing positive things about what you're doing with the kids. Thanks for your hard work."

Abby managed to mumble something in response. As he left, she sat at one of the tables. Mikayla had lost her home within weeks of her *daed*'s tragic death? Why hadn't David told Abby? He must have, like Glen, assumed she already knew. Thinking of the meeting they'd had in Glen's office weeks ago, she recalled the project manager mentioning how they'd be soon choosing the next houses to be built. Not once had she imagined one of the houses might replace Mikayla's home.

Tears filled her eyes as she bent her head to pray for strength for the girl who'd lost even more than Abby had imagined. She asked God to guide her in helping the girl by being able to listen to Mikayla's needs and fears and doubts.

As she murmured an "Amen," she opened her eyes to see Mikayla crossing the room toward her. "Mikayla, what are you doing here now? You should be at school."

"I know, but I need to talk to you about something." The girl hesitated. "Something important."

"Of course. Anytime." *God, I ask for Your help for this moment. Please be here for both of us.*

Mikayla glanced at the bustling kitchen. "Can we talk somewhere else?"

"How about we talk while I walk to school with you?"

The teen nodded and stepped aside as Abby went to collect her coat and bonnet. Going out into the spring day, Abby admired the crocus blossoms and the spikes of daffodils pushing their way up through the softening ground, but turned her attention to the girl beside her.

Mikayla glanced around again to make sure

nobody else stood too close, though the street was empty except for them. She leaned forward to whisper, "I don't like David's parents."

"You've just met them."

The teen grimaced. "Don't tell me to give them a chance to show their true selves. I've already seen them." She folded her arms in front of her and glowered at the sidewalk. "I don't like them, and they don't like me."

Abby resisted saying she understood why Mikayla felt as she did. Abby's own first impressions of David's parents continued to disturb her.

"I won't tell you to give them a chance," Abby said as they crossed the street and stepped onto the green. "They're going to be a part of your life because they're David's *mamm* and *daed*."

"So I need to grin and bear it when they tell me everything I do and say and how I look is wrong."

"Everything?"

Mikayla's scowl lessened by a few degrees. "Well, maybe not *everything*. I'm not doing anything wrong when I breathe."

Chuckling, Abby put her hand on the girl's stiff shoulder. "Then breathe when you're around them. Don't bristle in frustration. Don't talk back. Don't glare at them. Breathe and be grateful God's given you a chance to see how *wunderbaar* most things are in your life."

"You make it sound easy. To be honest, if I had anywhere else to go, I would." She didn't pause before she blurted, "How can someone like me become someone like you?"

Abby stared at the teen. *Someone like her?* Mikayla didn't want to be like her, living her life in the shadows of events that had happened almost a decade before.

"What do you mean when you say 'someone like you?'" Abby asked.

"Amish, of course."

Abby was shocked speechless. She hadn't expected the girl to say *that*! "Why are you interested in becoming Amish?" She let a hint of levity into her voice. "I know it's not because of the clothes. I've seen you and your friends giggle about what we wear."

Mikayla gave her a shy grin. "I'm sorry about that."

"No need to apologize. God wants us to be honest with one another because that helps us be more honest with Him."

"And *that* is why I want to be Amish!"

"I don't understand."

"Your faith isn't something you talk about on Sundays. It's something you live every minute of every day."

Abby took the girl's hand and led her to a bench by a tree. Sitting, she drew Mikayla down beside her. She swiveled on the bench so she could look at the teen.

"Mikayla," she said, hoping she was striking the right balance between stern and sympathetic, "I can see you're not being honest with me. What's the real reason you're asking about becoming Amish?"

The girl's eyes cut away toward the far side of the village green. "You're a family. You told me your grandparents live in the house with the rest of your family."

"*Ja*, they live with my cousins in Pennsylvania."

"And you've got a new stepmother, but you don't resent her."

"Why would I resent Lovina? She's kind, and she makes *Daed* happy. He was sad and lonely with only his *kinder* around."

Mikayla lifted off her glasses and knuckled her eyes, but tears bubbled at their corners. "I miss being part of a family."

"You *are* part of a family. A small one, but you and David are a family." She leaned forward and put her hand over the girl's. "Have you talked to him about this?"

"Not exactly."

"*Not exactly* means *no*, ain't so?"

The teen nodded.

"You asked me what I think," Abby said, "and

I think you and David need to talk. Honestly. David was your *daed*'s best friend for years and years. Your *daed* named David as your guardian."

More tears erupted from the girl, and she hid her face in her hands, pushing her glasses to an odd angle. "I know that, Abby."

Pulling Mikayla's hands away from her face, she looked the tearful *kind* in the eyes as she straightened Mikayla's glasses. "As long as you keep putting up walls between you and David, you won't have the family you long for."

She lowered her head and her long, silken hair pooled on her lap. "I don't want David to be my father."

"Why?" Abby asked, shocked. "He cares for you."

"I can't. Okay? Can't we leave it at that?"

Though Abby knew she should say no, she whispered, "Of course."

"Why can't I become Amish and then everyone will be part of my family? I won't do—" She halted her words and swallowed hard as she wrapped her arms around herself and shuddered. "It'd be easier."

So many things Abby wanted to ask because the girl acted as if some horrible, dark cloud hung over her, but Abby held her tongue. Guiding the girl toward an answer was all she could do. She couldn't make up Mikayla's mind for her. She wondered if she should speak of what Glen had told her about David arranging to have Mikayla's home rebuilt. The project manager wanted to talk to David before Mikayla was informed. There must be a reason for that, and Abby didn't want to make the situation more difficult.

Once Mikayla had pulled herself together, the teen headed to school.

Abby returned to the kitchen. Without a word to anyone, she picked up the phone and called David.

As soon as he said hello, she said, "David, this is Abby."

"Abby! Is something wrong?"

"No. I wasn't sure where you'd be working today, and I wanted to invite you and Mikayla and your parents to join us tonight at the community center for supper."

There was a long pause before he said, "I don't think that's a good idea."

"Maybe not, but you need to come here tonight. That way your parents can meet more of our volunteers, not just the Amish ones."

Again time stretched before he replied, "I'll ask them. I'm not making any promises."

"Of course not, but I'm sure Mikayla would like

them to meet her friends. It might create a stronger connection between your parents and her."

This time he didn't hesitate. "Now *that* is a good idea. Thanks, Abby. I'll see you this evening. Around six, right?"

"That'll be *gut. Danki*, David."

She hung up the phone, praying she'd done the right thing.

David half anticipated his parents to balk at the community center door, but when he held it open, they followed Mikayla into the main room. It was bustling with an expanded group of volunteers who'd come to start the next projects. He glanced with guilt at Mikayla. He hadn't said anything to her about Glen's call to let him know the St. Pierre house could be among the next raised out of the mud left by the flood. Glen had said he needed a decision by the end of next week, so David was delaying it until after his parents left in a few days for Old Orchard Beach in Maine.

After putting their coats on one of the many pegs along the wall, his parents hung back as they faced the noisy, jubilant crowd celebrating that a roof had been completed a few hours ago. Mikayla wove her way through as she looked for her friends. Or was she trying to get away from his parents who'd critiqued everything she'd said and done since their arrival? Though he'd asked them to stop, they continued to harangue the girl.

Odd, but he never would have guessed he'd see his parents and Abby's brother as similar, but both seemed intent on having the world match their image of what it should be. They'd been as exacting with him as they were trying to be with Mikayla. Maybe, he realized with astonishment, that was why he'd tried to give his daughter her space. Had he gone too far in the other direction in his attempt not to be the type of parent his own had been?

"If we want to eat," David said, motioning to the queue of people snaking among the tables, "we should get in line."

"No hurry," his mother said. "We can wait, can't we, Ed?"

"Yes," his father replied, "let the others who've worked hard go first."

Puzzled because his father had mentioned how hungry he was several times, David offered to introduce his parents to Glen and some of the other volunteers. Again, they demurred, seeming happy to cling to their corner where they could talk to each other.

He excused himself when Michael Miller motioned to him. Michael was sitting with his soon-to-be family at a table not far from the pass-through window. Smiling a greeting to Michael's fiancée and children, David congratulated his friend on getting the roof up on the house his team was building.

"It's a *gut* feeling to have that important step done with April showers coming and going." Michael put down his fork. "I was wondering if you could stop by tomorrow or the next day and check on the furnace before we fire it up the first time. Just to make sure we've gotten the connections right."

"Be glad to." He done the same for each of the previous houses. He hadn't found any problems, but he appreciated Michael's sense of caution. "Any time better for you?"

"Whenever you want to stop by."

"Sounds good." His smile wavered when he saw Abby walking toward him. He was glad she hadn't expected him to apologize for kissing her, because he wasn't sorry he had. But since then, nothing had been the same between them.

She refilled Michael's cup with what she assured him was decaf. "David, let your folks know that they can get in line at any time."

"They told me that the people who've worked hard today should have first dibs on the food."

"How kind of them, but let them know we made enough to feed everyone at a mud sale."

He recognized the term from some memory

that had been lying quiescent. A mud sale was an auction held in the spring, usually a fund-raiser for a school or a local volunteer fire department. The term *mud sale* had come about because when the sales were held, the earth was no longer frozen and spring rains often turned the grounds around a barn into a quagmire.

More and more as he spent time with Abby, the bits of his past that he'd stashed into a deep corner of his mind were springing to life again. So many were happy memories, and he wondered why he'd pushed them away.

That, he knew with abrupt insight, was easy. He hadn't wanted to upset his parents who had been distraught at whatever had driven them from their Amish lives. Even a young child knew when something caused a parent anguish and would do whatever was necessary to avoid it.

Abby picked up another empty cup and filled it. When she handed it to him, he said, "I don't like decaf."

"Sorry." She leaned toward him and lowered her voice. "We need to talk. It's important, David." She glanced at his daughter. "Really important."

"Can it wait until tomorrow? With my parents here…" He didn't finish and he guessed he didn't have to because understanding bloomed in her eyes.

"I guess it'll have to. I'll see you then."

Though he wanted to ask her what was wrong, he didn't. Mikayla was unhappy with his parents in the house, and he hoped that was what Abby wanted to discuss. He didn't want to think what other difficulties might lurk in his troubled relationships.

The community center was wrapped in dusk when Abby heard the door open. In astonishment, she saw David skulk into the kitchen. Why was he back now? He'd said they'd talk tomorrow. What had changed his mind?

Earlier, she'd watched him with his standoffish *daed* and *mamm*. They'd sat by themselves and had spoken only when someone stopped by their table to talk to David. When they'd dawdled over their meal, making the kitchen volunteers wait to clean their dishes after the others had been done, she'd been surprised. She'd assumed they'd duck out quickly. Were their unfriendly ways the reason David hadn't spoken much about them? That didn't make sense, because she'd seen that he had affection for them in an almost protective way, as if they were the *kinder* and he the parent.

"Kaffi?" she asked instead of the questions pounding against her lips.

"No, thanks. You said we needed to talk

about something important. Something about Mikayla?"

She gestured for him to follow her to one of the tables in the dimly lit main room. Sitting, she waited until he chose a seat facing her. The distance between them seemed too intimate and too vast at the same time.

He listened without comment as she outlined the conversation she'd had with Mikayla earlier. Leaning back in his chair, he sat so his face was too shadowed for her to read his reaction.

"She's hurting, David, and she doesn't know where else to turn. She wants to have a family, but she seems scared of making one with you."

"Scared?"

"*Ja.* For some reason she believes it'd be different if she lived a plain life. I didn't want to discourage her, but she sees living as we do a panacea for her grief."

"I can think of a sure way to change her mind." His voice coming out of the shadows was grim.

"What is it?"

"I can tell her the truth."

"The truth? The truth about what?"

"Me. Me and my parents."

Now he had baffled her because she opened her mouth to ask another question, but no sound emerged. She took a deep breath and released it before she asked, "Why would the truth about your family have anything to do with her thinking she wants to live a plain life?"

"Because we used to be Amish."

Chapter Fifteen

Understanding how a fish felt out of water, Abby gasped for air. A whooshing grew loud, then receded in her ears. Her voice sounded weird as she asked, "You—you were Amish?"

"Until I was around five or six years old." He slanted toward her and she could see his face was as dreary as his voice. "I don't remember exactly how old because my parents took me away a couple of times before we left for good."

"So you remember that life?" She couldn't believe she was as poised as if he were talking about something no more surprising than how Tuesday followed Monday each week.

"Very little. When I was that age, I did pretty much the same things that any child does. I played with my friends and cousins, enjoyed time and meals with my parents as well as having someone tuck me in at night and read me a story."

"*Ja*, in those ways plain and *Englisch kinder* are much the same." She paused. "Is that why you understand some *Deitsch*?"

"Maybe. I don't know." He rubbed his eyes, then raised them to meet her gaze. "I've understood a few words when you spoke them, but it may have been because they sound like English or I could figure out the meaning through context. My parents stopped speaking *Deitsch*, so I'd thought I'd forgotten it. I know what you're going to ask next. Why did my parents leave?"

She nodded.

"I'm not sure."

Abby was shocked to the depths of her soul. As curious as David was about everything around him, a trait that had led him to learn about how machines worked so he could repair them, she'd expected him to have a quick answer to soothe *her* curiosity about why he and his parents had walked away from their plain community.

She wanted to put her hands up to the sides of her head to make sure it was still in place. With every thought, her mind spun like a mixer set at highest speed. It was difficult to believe she was sitting instead of floating around like a runaway kite.

David had been born plain? He did live a simple life, but so did many of the people in Evergreen Corners.

Then she thought of his parents. Nothing about them had suggested they'd ever been Amish. They wore *Englisch* clothing. Their hair was cut in *Englisch* styles. His *mamm* had been draped in elegant jewelry each time Abby had seen her, and she wore those stilettos Abby couldn't imagine trying to walk in. His *daed* wore a thick gold watch and a mustache. If someone had asked, she would have said the closest they might have ever been to plain folk was visiting the tourist shops in Pennsylvania.

And David… Nothing about how he dressed suggested he'd ever worn broadfall trousers and suspenders and a straw hat with a narrow black band.

"Are you from Pennsylvania, too?" she asked, struggling to enunciate each word because her lips were trembling so hard.

"I'm not sure where we lived before my folks left."

"Your birth certificate—"

"It lists my birth place as Sugarcreek, Ohio, but I do recall that we moved several times before we came here. Once we settled in Evergreen Corners, we never went to visit family again. I don't remember my grandparents' faces, though I sometimes recall hints of their voices."

"Oh, my," she whispered. "Now I understand why your parents jumped the fence."

"Jumped the fence?"

"That means leaving the Amish, and I'd guess your parents did because they were under the *bann*," she whispered. "That's why they ate last and made sure their dishes were the final ones washed tonight."

"I don't have any idea what you're talking about."

"Do you know what 'under the *bann*' means?"

"No." His eyes narrowed. "Are you talking about being shunned?"

"*Ja.* When an Amish person does something that violates the rules of the *Ordnung*, they are shunned."

"Kicked out, you mean? Told to hit the road because they refused to kowtow to rules set by a bunch of old men? I don't understand how a people who preach kindness and nonviolence can treat their own that way. How can kicking someone out of their home be part of Jesus's teachings?"

She wanted to recoil from the venom in his voice but forced hers to remain calm. "That's a misconception many *Englischers* have. Being put under the *bann* isn't an act of retribution. It's an act of love."

"Do you believe that?" he asked with a snort.

"Ja." She leaned across the table and put her hands on his, not caring what she was risking by touching him. He needed to know the truth to deal with the pain that had been a part of him for more than two decades. "David, listen to me. Being under the *bann* means you aren't part of the faith community until you confess your sin. It's a loving act that gives the sinner a chance to see what would be lost and what can be regained if he or she will set aside their *hochmut*—their pride—and admit their wrongdoing. No one is forced to leave their home and their community, but they must eat separately and nothing must pass from their hands to ours. Your parents took their food last and had their dishes washed last, so what have been labeled as their sins wouldn't contaminate the rest of the community."

She was shocked anew the Riehls still clung to some of the beliefs they'd otherwise set aside. Or had they believed someone tonight would have pointed a finger at them, telling them they shouldn't eat with others because of the *bann*? Old habits were hard to break and old fears hard to set aside.

"Is ostracism any better than being kicked out?" David asked in the same razor-sharp tone.

"No, it's not. I had an *onkel* who was put under the *bann* for two weeks because he bet on football games. It was sad when he couldn't sit at the table with us and share in God's grace and bounty. His business didn't suffer because he was under the *bann*. During that time, his customers left money on the counter in his small engine shop so it didn't pass from their hands to his."

"So he knuckled under to the rules in two weeks?"

"He was put under the *bann* for two weeks, and at the end of that time, he was invited to rejoin us during our worship service to confess to his sins. Sometimes there is a specific time limit. In other situations, it's up to the person who's sinned to decide when or if to return." She gave his hand a light squeeze. "David, stop thinking of the *bann* as a punishment. The *bann* is a way for people to come to terms with their mistakes and for the *Leit* to understand the value of forgiveness. We must forgive those who trespass against us so we can be forgiven. Just as the Lord's Prayer teaches us."

"Apparently my parents got the permanent kind of shunning."

"They *chose* to let the shunning become permanent." She sighed. "No, that's not right, either. They've allowed it to continue thus far. If they ever wished to return, they could confess and ask for forgiveness."

"And you're telling me that they'd get it." He withdrew his hand from beneath hers and snapped his fingers. "Just like that?"

"If the *Leit* believed their confession was sincere, *ja*, forgiveness would be offered just like that." She snapped her own fingers. "And the matter would never be spoken of again."

"People aren't like that. They don't forget."

"I didn't say anyone would forget. I said that the transgression would be forgiven. How can we expect God to forgive us and welcome us into His grace if we don't offer the same forgiveness to others?"

"They don't want what you Amish are offering."

She jerked as if he'd struck her. "Each of us must find our own path."

He stood and slid his chair beneath the table. "Now that you know the truth, maybe you can understand why you can't fix me."

"Fix you?"

"Isn't that what you've been trying to do since you realized I'm Mikayla's guardian?"

"No!" She jumped to her feet.

He shook his head. "I never thought I'd see

the day you wouldn't be honest with me, Abby. You know as well as I do that you've been trying to fix everything you think is wrong with me. You've tried to prove I can be fun. You've done everything in your power to smooth the differences between Mikayla and me." Bitterness filled his voice as he added, "Now you can see I've got more problems than even you can fix."

"I'm not trying to fix you." She wanted to stamp her foot, but refused to behave like a *kind*. One of them needed to be the adult in the conversation and David was showing it wouldn't be him. "I'm trying to help you."

"What's the difference?"

"There's a huge difference. If I were trying to fix you, it would be because I think there's something wrong with you. Helping you means I see you have a need for someone to offer assistance. That's a big difference."

"I don't see it."

She bit back the words burning in her throat. Instead, she took a steadying breath. "That's apparent, but you're avoiding one vital fact."

"And you're going to tell me what it is."

Again she was tempted to tell him if he was going to act like a toddler, she couldn't see any point in continuing their heated conversation. She couldn't—she shouldn't—lambast him for his obstinacy when he was hurting.

"You know what it is, David. Not knowing why your parents left has been tearing you apart since the first plain volunteers arrived in Evergreen Corners. Before that, you could believe the Amish were the cruel, intractable people your parents taught you we are. You need to know the truth."

He opened his mouth to answer but halted when a shout exploded into the community center.

"Abby! Abby, where are you? Mikayla is gone!"

At Reece's shout, Abby exchanged a horrified glance with David. He flipped on the lights, and Reece and the other teens—the *Englisch* ones and the Amish ones—came to a stop in a squeal of sneaker soles.

"Here I am. What…?" Her voice trailed away.

The kids' expressions ranged from despair to fear to overt terror. Lily had tearstains running through the makeup on her cheeks as she clung to Jack. The other teens were wringing their hands as they looked to Reece, who had become the spokesman for the group.

"Mikayla's gone!" Reece shouted again.

"What do you mean?" Abby asked. "Gone where?"

"That's it. I—we don't know where she's gone."

Abby shook the niggling tendrils of panic out

of her mind. She couldn't let the kids' dismay infect her. She needed facts.

"Where was she when you last saw her?" David asked from behind Abby.

She glanced at him. Their gazes caught and locked for a brief second, but it was enough for her to know he agreed their problems must be set aside until they knew Mikayla was okay.

"I saw…" Reece hesitated, glanced at the other kids, then hurried to add, "I saw Mikayla a half hour ago with Hunter."

"With *Hunter*? Hunter Keyes?" Abby could barely believe her own words. "Why would she go with the boy who's been harassing you for weeks?"

Reece shrugged with a nonchalance that didn't match the strain in his voice. "I don't know. I saw the two of them walking together. I was going to follow to make sure he didn't do anything more to hurt her, but Glen wanted to talk to me. By the time I'd explained to him why I had to go, both of them were gone."

"Hunter is sixteen, ain't so?"

"Yes, but his car is in the parking lot. They must have walked somewhere."

"Where?" asked David, the strain to keep his voice calm was obvious in the single word.

"We don't know," cried Cindi as tears washed down her face. "I wanted to call the cops, but

Jack—" She glared at him as if everything that had happened was his fault. "Jack said we should talk to you first. That you'd know the best thing to do."

Reece looked distraught. "Sending the cops after them might make things worse." His voice broke on the last word and color sprang up his face.

"How?"

Before anyone could answer Abby's question, Dwight elbowed his way to the front of the group of teens. "I think I know why she went with him."

"Why?" she asked, again fighting the panic roiling through her.

"She was talking at supper about how we need to forgive those who treat us bad. While we can. That's what she said. We have to forgive them while we can."

Abby turned to David. "Do you know why she was talking about that today?"

He nodded. "We had a big discussion about the importance of asking and giving forgiveness at our house last night." His gaze locked with Abby's. "A big discussion."

"Or," Reece said, "she wants to hang out with him rather than with us, and this gave her the excuse."

"No!" Abby didn't care that all eyes turned

on her. "I understand how going with a bad boy because he's a bit dangerous can seem enticing, but it's a road to trouble."

"What are you talking about?" David asked.

She waved aside his question, realizing how much she'd almost revealed. "We don't have time to talk about what happened years ago." What would he think of her when he learned how foolish and selfish she'd been? Now, more than ever, she needed to follow her common sense and let her breaking heart fend for itself. "We need to find Mikayla."

David gathered the teens around him and peppered them with questions. Reece, Jack and Cindi were his daughter's closest friends. It was possible they knew something they weren't aware of, the very thing that could lead them to Mikayla.

Two minutes later his hopes were dashed. Reece was the only one who'd seen Mikayla with Hunter, and he hadn't seen where they were headed. Dividing up the kids, David sent them to several of the spots where Mikayla might have gone while he headed to their house to check if she'd shown up there. He directed Jack to find Michael and ask him to round up more help. He told them to have everyone report in at the community center in an hour. What he didn't say was if there wasn't any sign of her by then, he'd alert the authorities.

"I'll stay here," Abby said. "If someone finds Mikayla and Hunter, I'll have one of the *Englischers* send out a text message to Jack's phone. He can alert everyone else."

It was a good plan, but as minutes passed and ten became twenty, then forty, the kids found nothing in the usual places where teens hung out. David's house was empty. His parents must have gone somewhere after supper. He pushed aside his irritation at how they kept him out of the loop of their lives. He needed to concentrate on finding his daughter. Leaving a note on the kitchen table for Mikayla to call him, he wondered where the two kids had gone. Was his daughter okay?

As he returned to the community center, it started to rain. A cold, wintry rain that warned they'd been foolish to think spring had arrived. He ducked his head into it, hoping it wouldn't turn to sleet as the night grew colder.

The community center was a hubbub of activity. He slipped in and saw Michael talking with Isaac. Abby's brother had pulled out a map of the area and was asking questions. David looked for Abby and saw her pouring coffee. Her face was set in determined lines, but he saw the ravages of worry gouged into her cheeks.

"Glen has talked to the police," she said after she wound her way through the crowd to get to him. "They can't do much until a full day has passed, but will keep an eye out for Mikayla and Hunter."

A full day? He couldn't live through twenty-three more hours of not knowing where his daughter was.

Working with Michael and Isaac and other volunteers, David helped make up assignments. The volunteers were about to dash out the door to widen the search, when it opened. He heard a few gasps, including one of his own, but nobody spoke as Mikayla, wearing her light blue spring coat, walked in alongside Hunter Keyes.

The boy aimed a hostile stare at everyone. He raised his clenched hands when David jumped forward.

David paid the boy no attention. He grabbed his daughter by the shoulders and pulled her into a quick embrace. "Mikayla, you're okay!"

"Why wouldn't I be?" she asked, wiggling away.

He released her and frowned at Hunter. "You know why, Mikayla."

With his chin raised in a defiant pose, the boy growled, "Yeah, he thinks I'm going to do something bad to you, Mick."

When Reece bristled at the other boy's familiarity, David put a hand on each boy's shoulder.

"Okay, enough of this posturing." He turned to the rest of the room. "Thank you."

The crowd quickly dispersed, happy the kids were safe. Soon, only the teens and Abby stood with David in the main room. He was surprised when Hunter didn't leave with everyone else.

Reece must have been, too, because he snarled, "Some people don't know when they're not welcome."

When Hunter clenched his hands again, David said, "There's no need for anybody to antagonize anyone else."

Hunter stepped away and folded his arms over his chest. "I don't need you telling me what I can or can't do. You're not my—"

"Hunter," Mikayla said, "you promised you'd be nice."

"I know." The boy hung his head, looking like a chastised puppy.

Disbelief appeared on the faces of the other teens, but before anyone else could speak, Abby urged them to sit. She carried a tray of brownies from the kitchen to the largest round table and pulled out a chair.

David waited until each of the kids had chosen a chair, Hunter last of all, before he pulled out one for himself. "Okay, Mikayla, what's going on? You had everyone worried when you went off without telling anyone where you were going."

"I'm sorry to worry you, but I'm doing what Abby taught me to do."

"What's that?" He glanced at Abby, who obviously had no more idea than he did what Mikayla was talking about.

His daughter gave him a lopsided smile. "She didn't come out and tell me, but I've seen how when she makes a mistake, she apologizes and then lets it go. She doesn't dwell on it. Her mistake doesn't take over her life. That's how the Amish are. They forgive."

He was surprised when he saw Abby flinch. Something about Mikayla's words had pricked her. But what? Did it have something to do with what she'd said about her past before she'd clammed up?

Even if he'd known how to ask, he didn't have a chance because his parents walked into the community center. David looked from Abby's distraught eyes to his parents' furious ones. Why had they come now? He had his answer when his father tossed a piece of paper on the table. It was, David saw, the note he'd written to let Mikayla know he was looking for her.

"The Amish forgive?" His mother sneered at Abby. "What lies have you been feeding these children along with your brownies?"

Chapter Sixteen

David ignored the shocked teens as he stood. Lifting the paper off the table, he said, "I would have thought your first concern, after seeing this, would be for Mikayla."

"She's right there." Without another word, his father picked up a pair of gloves from beneath the pegs where they'd hung their coats earlier.

David wondered how much of the conversation his parents had heard. It hadn't been that long ago when he warned Abby how his mother liked to eavesdrop.

"Don't listen to that woman," Mother said with the same icy disdain. "She's filling your heads with nonsense."

He heard the teens shift in their chairs. They were too polite to call out his mother, but they didn't like hearing Abby insulted.

"It's not nonsense, Mother. Abby is helping these young people learn to live a better life."

"A life that doesn't have anything to do with us."

For a moment, he was speechless. Why did his parents think the conversation was about them? Then he understood. Guilt. They carried the same burden he did, but did so knowingly.

Facing his parents, he said, "How would I know that? You've never answered my questions about why you left the Amish."

That brought big gasps from the kids. From the corner of his eye, he saw Abby trying to hush them, but he kept his gaze locked with his parents'.

"We have answered your questions," his mother asserted. "Every single one, haven't we, Ed?"

"Every single one."

David drew in a steadying breath before he said something he'd regret. After years of trying to discover the truth, he'd come to recognize the tricks his parents used to divert him. They agreed with each other, always parroting the other's words, to take over the conversation and steer it where they wanted it to go.

"Then tell me again now that I'm an adult and can understand it."

His parents exchanged an uneasy look then his mother glared at Abby.

"This is a private family matter."

"No," he argued.

Abby interjected to say, "We can leave, David."

David faced her. He couldn't mistake the gentle warmth in her gaze. He didn't want her to go. She was the only one on his side. He froze at the thought, wondering when sides had been chosen and why he was on a different one than his parents.

"Stay, Abby. I can't go on being torn apart between what I used to believe and what you and the others have shown me with your hard work and concern for Evergreen Corners."

When fingers grasped his hand, he looked down to see Mikayla's worried face. With a renewed shock, as if he'd grabbed hold of a live wire, he remembered that the whole discussion about his past had begun because his daughter had approached Abby about becoming Amish. Because she wanted to be part of a family as much as he did?

Standing, Mikayla motioned to her friends. They got up and walked away. The kitchen door closed behind them and then the pass-through window was shut.

"I can go with them," Abby whispered.

"Stay. Please." His voice broke as Reece's had earlier.

"*Ja.* For as long as you want me to."

Her words resonated in his mind. She'd stay for as long as he wanted her to? Was she saying what he hoped she was saying?

He couldn't think of that now. "Tell me the truth," he said as he looked at his parents again.

His father spoke first. "You shouldn't ask your mother to recount what happened again."

"It isn't again. You two have never explained to me why you left the Amish and cut off connections with them. Look. I want to know the truth. I don't want to judge you or what happened to you. What happened to *us.* I want to know what happened."

"We'd hoped you wouldn't remember those days," his mother said with a sigh as she shrank into her coat.

"I don't remember much. Or I didn't until the plain volunteers came to help rebuild Evergreen Corners."

"That woman has twisted your mind." Her nose wrinkled as she glared at Abby.

He wanted to step between Abby and his mother's scowl, but he knew Abby understood his mother's pain. "She isn't the only Amish person I know."

"But the most important," his mother argued. With her face so pale that every bit of her makeup looked garish, she blinked. Was she trying not to cry? He wanted to apologize that his quest for the truth was bringing her pain.

God, there must be a way for me to know what happened without adding to what they've already suffered. Help me find it.

"Please tell me why you left," he pleaded.

"I suppose he has a right to know, Ed." His mother folded and unfolded her hands as if weaving an invisible garment. "It's part of his history, too."

"Some history should be forgotten." His father wasn't willing to budge an inch.

"Please, Ed."

His father's face crumpled, and David couldn't help wondering if his father was sending up a similar prayer of his own. Wishing he knew which Bible verse stated "the truth shall make you free," David kept his lips closed. He suspected anything he said now would add to his parents' wretchedness.

"All right, Nora. If you want to leave, I can…"

She shook her head and squared her shoulders. "It's my story, too."

David bit his lower lip as he looked from his father to his mother. The love that had knit them together had grown stronger through the years, and he wondered if that was, in part, because they'd felt they were alone in the world except for their only child.

His father sat at the table and clasped his hands on it, his knuckles bleached with tension. "We lived as Amish youth should. We met at a singing on a Sunday evening, and I asked your mother to let me take her home in my buggy that night. After that, she rode in my buggy every other Sunday after singings, and I often drove over to her parents' house on Saturday nights to take her to other youth events in the area. I asked her to be my wife, and she agreed. We were baptized. And then we were married, and a couple of years later, you were born."

"I thought—" He took care this time not to mention Abby's name. "I thought when you chose baptism, you agreed to follow the rules of your district's *Ordnung.*"

"You've learned a lot about plain ways. Has *that* woman—"

He refused to let either of them disparage Abby again. "For the past five months, a lot of Amish volunteers have come to Evergreen Corners to help those who need them most. They've welcomed us with food and with their skills and with their kindness, lifting us up when we were at our lowest."

"Your property wasn't flooded," his mother interjected.

"No, it wasn't, but Mikayla's was." When his parents looked confused, he explained how the St. Pierre house had been destroyed. "It was empty because she was at my house, but it was her home. Her last connection with her father. Now it's gone. That has nothing to do with any of this. Why did you jump the fence?"

His parents looked at each other again then his father said, "Because your mother was accused of something she didn't do."

"What?" He glanced at his mother, who was looking everywhere but at him. "I'm sorry, but I need to know."

"Our bishop's wife had it in for your mother, and she accused your mother of wearing clothing that didn't fit with the rules set forth by the *Ordnung*."

Some strong emotion raced through his mother's eyes, but it wasn't regret. In that instant he knew the accusation had been honest. Why would they give up their families and friends for such a small misdemeanor?

He got his answer when his father said, "*Daed*—who was our bishop—refused to step in to say your mother wasn't wrong."

"That's because," his mother said bitterly,

"he was afraid of his wife. She wanted us to be afraid of her, but I refused to be."

David felt as if he'd run headlong into a wall. A disagreement between his mother and his grandmother had created a fissure that had torn the family apart. Two proud women—both of whom would deny their *hochmut*, as Abby called it—had put being right above everything else.

Something released from around his heart. For so long, he'd cradled his guilt as if it were a precious gift. It wasn't. It had fooled him into believing *he* had been the reason his parents had left their Amish family. Instead of bringing his guilt out into the light of reality, he'd empowered it, giving it more strength to torture him.

"Why didn't you ask for forgiveness?" he asked.

"Why didn't *she*?" his mother fired back.

"If you'd asked, wouldn't it have been granted to you? And couldn't you have forgiven her?"

His mother yanked the door open. "Come, Ed. It's time we left where we're not wanted any longer."

David tried to halt her by reassuring them that they'd misunderstood his need to know the truth. Nothing changed their minds or their dramatic exit into the rainy night. The hurt was too old, too deeply ingrained, he realized, to be soothed with common sense.

Arms curved around his shoulders and he bent to put his cheek on Abby's *kapp*. Neither of them spoke, but he knew all her thoughts were for him and his family.

"I'm so—" Her words were lost beneath an abrupt crash.

Running to the door, he threw it open. He took a single look and sped toward the car that had hit a tree at the lower end of the village green. Already fire licked the car's undercarriage.

His parents' car.

Abby called after him, but he didn't slow on the icy road. More shouts came from every direction. People appeared out of the dark. By the time he'd reached the car, others were there, too.

He grabbed the driver's-side door. His fingers were seared. Jerking them back, he pulled down his coat sleeve to cover his hand and tried again. He could see his father, slumped into the air bag.

The door wouldn't open.

Someone shoved a crowbar into his hand. Grabbing it, he shifted his grip to let others seize it, too. He slid it around the door and shouted, "Now!"

Sirens rang as he put his whole weight along

with the other two men holding on to the bar. The metal peeled back, but not far enough.

Yanking the crowbar out of their hands, he raised it and slammed it against the window. Glass shattered as the flames near his feet threatened to melt his boots. He used the bar to sweep the shards aside and reached inside. He couldn't reach the seat belt release.

"Move!" shouted Isaac from behind him. "I'll cut him loose."

He obeyed, and Abby's brother sliced through the seat belt with a sharp knife. As the pieces fell away, David and Isaac tugged his father through the window. Other arms appeared out of the sleet to cradle his father so he didn't fall into the strengthening fire.

"Got him!" someone called. "What about Mrs. Riehl?"

David whirled to go around to the far side of the car, but saw another group of people, this one including Abby, carrying his mother away from the car. He breathed a grateful prayer.

The rescue squad and the fire trucks arrived at the same moment. While the firemen pumped water from the brook onto the car, his parents were lifted with care into the ambulance. An EMT told David, while putting salve on his burnt hand and wrapping it, that each of his parents had a broken arm and possibly a concussion from the air bags.

"Go home and put some dry clothes on before you come over to the hospital," the man said. "The ER staff won't let you in for at least a half an hour, so take your time on the slippery roads."

He nodded and stepped aside as the ambulance pulled out with care, not wanting to risk another accident.

"This is my fault," he said into the darkness.

From behind them, Mikayla cried, "No! Don't say that."

Abby moved to put her arms around the distraught girl. As she led the girl and David up onto a nearby porch so they were out of the rain, Mikayla repeated, "No, David! Don't say that!" The teen didn't wipe away her tears as her friends followed them onto the porch. "Abby, tell him what you told me about not letting guilt rule your life as it has mine."

David stared at her. "Guilt? What do you have to feel guilty about?"

"About Dad's death."

Reece grasped her hand. "You weren't driving."

"I've never told anyone but Hunter, because

he understands." She shuddered as a police car slowed to a cautious stop by the fire trucks.

Had it looked like this the night Boyd St. Pierre had died? Abby saw the same question in David's eyes, but neither of them spoke.

"The day of the accident," Mikayla went on, "I wanted to go to a big sale in Brattleboro. Dad said the roads were too icy, and we'd go next week. The sale would have been over by then." She faltered but continued when Hunter climbed the stairs to stand a short distance away. "I whined and I pouted and threw a fit until Dad got tired of listening to me. He told me he'd take me. I walked away with bruises. Dad didn't."

She put her head into her hands and wept.

When her girlfriends moved to console her, Abby held them back. The boys looked overwhelmed and unsure.

David enfolded Mikayla in his arms. She clung to him as if she were a little girl. He pulled a handkerchief from his pocket and handed it to her.

After she wiped her face and blew her nose, she said between the hiccupping remnants of her sobs, "I'm sorry, David."

"You've got nothing to be sorry for."

"I've been horrible to you. I know you've been mourning Dad's death, too, but I couldn't add another person's pain to mine, so I shut you out."

"I understand," he said. "Sometimes it's easier to create a shell around yourself and your pain than to have to face the rest of the world. I was doing that, too…at least for a while." He looked at Abby. "Lately my faith has grown stronger, and I've been reaching out to our Heavenly Father to guide me through the shadows."

"If it hadn't been for me, Dad—"

"It was an accident. Nothing you did caused it. Nothing you do now can change it." He bent so his eyes were level with hers. "Here are a couple of things I want you to remember, Mikayla St. Pierre. Your father loved you more than anything or anyone in the whole world. Because he loved you so much, he wouldn't want you to spend your whole life filled with guilt for something that wasn't your fault."

"If I hadn't begged and pouted—"

"Listen to me." He held her gaze, not letting her look away. "It was an accident, and Boyd wasn't at fault. You weren't, either. Nobody was. That's why we call it an accident."

"But people were hurt!" Hunter protested, shocking Abby, who'd forgotten the erstwhile bully was there. "My uncle is in a wheelchair now because someone did something stupid."

"Your uncle was in the accident, too?" Abby asked.

"Yeah, and me, though I wasn't hurt. That's why Mick and I started talking when nobody else was around. If someone hadn't been stupid—"

"The police said more than one car lost control on the ice to cause the pileup," David said.

"And would you feel better," asked Abby as she moved next to Hunter, who towered over her, "if you had the name of someone to blame? Would it change what happened to your uncle? Would it erase your own memories of that night?" She put her fingers on his fist.

She didn't try to pry his fingers open. She prayed he'd find comfort in her touch.

"If you want to blame someone," she went on, "blame God. He loves us enough to let us do that. Go to Him and lay down the burden of your pain and grief at His feet. He shares our pain, and you know, Hunter, a pain shared is a pain lessened. That's what you and Mikayla have been talking about, ain't so? She's come home crying, but not because you were bullying her, but because, together, you were sharing your pain. Now you must do the same with the guilt that seeks to consume both of you."

The teen stared at his boots, his jaw working as he tried to hold in his grief. She looked at David. Did he understand that her words for Hunter were for him, as well?

"Hunter," Abby continued gently, "we plain people learn one thing from the time we're *kinder*. We learn we must forgive in order to be forgiven, whether it's forgiving and asking forgiveness from others or whether it's doing the same for ourselves." She turned to face Mikayla. "And learning to forgive ourselves is one of the hardest tasks we'll ever face."

The sound of weeping came from where Cindi and Lily stood, their arms around each other. The boys shuffled their feet, trying to keep their own emotions in check. Suddenly, Reece threw his arms around Mikayla, squeezing her as he said over and over how sorry he was he hadn't been able to help her.

When David cleared his throat, the boy released Mikayla. Reece wore a sheepish expression, but his face lit with a smile when David offered his hand. Shaking it, Reece nodded, too overcome to speak.

"Is finding forgiveness why you talked to Abby about becoming Amish, Mikayla?" David asked.

Hunter gasped. "You want to be Ay-mi…?" He glanced at Abby and then, lowering his eyes again, repeated the question as he pronounced the word correctly.

Instead of answering him, Mikayla said, "I wanted to become Amish because…" She dragged her hand across her face, smearing her makeup more. "I wanted to be Amish because they don't drive cars, so they don't get into accidents."

"That's not true," Abby whispered.

"What do you mean?" asked Mikayla.

"There are buggy crashes, too. Some are accidental. Some are…not. You asked me, David, about how I mentioned a *gut* girl could sometimes want to step out of line and do something a bit more adventurous."

"You said it was about the past," he said.

"It is. My past. Two buggies crashed while racing. Two young men's lives were changed forever, but it wasn't an accident. Nobody could blame the tragedy on an icy road. They'd both been drinking, and they both were angry." She met his eyes and saw compassion there. He would understand, because he knew how guilt could take over someone's life. Why hadn't she perceived that before? "They were angry because of me. I was expected to let one of them take me home but I went with the other. If I'd done as I should have to help one of them instead of doing what I wanted to do, the accident might never have happened."

"So?" Mikayla asked. "So what if one guy

thought you were going with him and you decided to go with the other? Neither of them owned you, so you could do as you wished. And did it have anything to do with you? No! They might have raced some other time if they hadn't that night, right?"

"I don't know." Abby delved into the deep well of her memories that she'd been avoiding since that awful night. "*Ja*, they might have. They'd been teasing and taunting each other for weeks about which one had the faster buggy. I'd forgotten that."

"Don't forget it again." Mikayla grasped Abby's hands and squeezed them. "That night, you were free to do what you chose to do. Just like I can spend time with Hunter, if I want to, though I know Reece gets upset because he thinks I'm putting myself in danger."

"If Reece gives you trouble…" Hunter began but then halted when the girl gave him a pointed gaze. "I'm sure you can handle it yourself."

"You're learning, Hunter." She patted his arm. "One of these days, you may turn into a human being."

When Reece held out his hand to Hunter, the erstwhile bully hesitated, then took it and pumped it.

Abby smiled as she hugged Mikayla. "*Danki*. Now you're teaching me. It's a lesson I won't forget." Putting her hand on David's arm, she said, "Let's go and see how your parents are. They're going to want to see you."

"Are you sure they will?"

"Ja," she said, though she wasn't.

Hours later, as the clocks showed a new day had begun, Abby pulled on her coat in the ER waiting room. Both of David's parents had been admitted to the hospital for observation because their concussions had left them dazed. One thing they did recall was the argument that had led to Ed Riehl driving too fast and striking the tree, though neither remembered the accident. They were so happy to be alive and see their son they wanted to put the argument behind them.

Abby guessed there would need to be further discussion among the family, but that could wait until the Riehls were healed. As she watched David reach for his gloves, she was flushed with gratitude that God had led them to the truth. What had happened in the past mattered far less than what the future held. Mikayla and Abby had been wrong to take the blame for tragedies on their own shoulders. Now she felt lighter than she had in years as she handed her sense of guilt over to God.

"Hunter isn't the only one who needs God's help," she said as David began to zip up his coat.

"His bullying friends—"

She put a finger to his lips. When he regarded her with astonishment, she said, "I'm talking about us. We need God's help every day to discover the truth that our human foibles prevent us from seeing. I need to learn what Mikayla says I taught her." She laughed as she shook her head in disbelief. "Somehow she figured out what *I* need to learn myself. I hope by watching her, she can be my teacher."

"Doesn't the Bible tell us to become as children?"

"*Ja*, but don't call Mikayla a *kind*. She wouldn't appreciate that."

"True."

Mikayla walked into the waiting room. Holding out her hand to David, she opened her fingers.

"Happy belated Easter." She held out a bright yellow plastic egg.

Or it once had been bright yellow. Now it was covered with glitter and gold stars and tiny pictures of what looked like the sap house they'd visited. They'd been pasted on in every possible direction until most of the egg was covered.

He balanced it on his palm. "Did you make this, Mikayla?"

The girl nodded. "Open it."

"Nothing's going to jump out, is it?"

Abby was amazed when Mikayla gave a quick laugh. What a beautiful sound it was!

When David twisted the plastic egg open, a smaller egg wrapped in foil dropped onto the chair beside him. He snatched it up before it could fall onto the floor.

"Dad and I always exchanged one egg on Easter morning," Mikayla said, her voice rough with emotion. "We made them to remind us of fun times we had together. I had fun the day we went up to the top of Quarry Mountain and to the sap house. It was fun because of you, David." She gave him a quick hug.

"Oh, my stars!" he breathed as Mikayla rushed out of the room saying she'd meet them at the truck. "She made me an egg like she used to do for Boyd?"

Abby smiled. "*Ja.* A special tradition she shares with her *daed.*"

"I'm not really her father."

"Maybe not by birth. She didn't give you the egg because you're a substitute for her *daed.* She wants you to know how much she appreciates what you've done for her."

"I haven't—"

"You've done more than you can guess, David. You've given her a home. You've listened to her when she wants to talk, and you've convinced her to open up when she's been afraid to."

"I think that's what *you* have done." He placed the egg on her palm and closed her fingers over it. "Not only for Mikayla, but for me, too. That's why I need to tell you that I love you, Abby Kauffman, and I want you to be my wife."

"Your wife?" Shock pierced her. "You know I can't marry—"

"An *Englischer*. I know, but I wasn't born *Englisch*, and I don't have to stay *Englisch*. If you'll have me, Abby, I'll relearn what I need to in order to live a plain life with you."

"Do you realize what you're saying?"

He nodded. "I know what I'm saying. I've been talking with Michael Miller. He's told me it wasn't easy, but he knows of a few other *Englischers* who have been baptized Amish. I'll have to give up my truck and my electricity, but my job is one other plain men do. It'll take time while I relearn the language and the customs. Will you help me, Abby, so we can spend our lives together?"

"Mikayla—"

"I doubt she was serious about living a plain life, but if she is, I'll support her in that decision. Boyd wanted her to be happy and have the life she wants. I do, too. She'll always have a home with me." He lifted her hand to his lips and gave it a gentle kiss. "With us?"

She faltered. Should she listen to *gut* sense or should she follow her heart into David's arms? As she saw the joy in his eyes dim when she didn't answer, she knew there could be only one response, though the way ahead of them could be fraught with many twists and turns. Just as her life had always been.

"Ja," she murmured. "With us. I love you, David, and I want to be your wife."

"That's all the incentive I need to do what I must to be the man I was born to be." He put his arms around her and held her close.

This time when his mouth found hers, she soared on the love that had grown between them, even before they'd been aware of it. As she melted into his kiss, Abby savored this one and couldn't wait for the next. She knew it would be that way for the rest of their lives together.

Epilogue

"Here she comes. Be quiet."

"Shh!"

Abby tried not to laugh as the teenagers were so loud in their attempts to warn the others to be silent. The front room was dark because the curtains on the windows had been drawn tight. They waited there, listening for the hesitant steps coming toward them.

"Why are the drapes closed?" asked an elderly voice.

Stepping forward, Abby smiled at Doris Blomgren. The old woman was almost recovered from the effects of her fall. Now that summer was in full bloom, she was able to get around her house with the help of a walker. She no longer lived alone, because her great-niece, Barbara, had moved in to help her remain in her home.

"We're done," Abby said with a broadening smile.

"Done?" Doris's eyes filled with happy tears. "With my... With the project?"

"Ja." Without turning, she said, "Open those drapes."

The teen group, which now included Hunter and one of his former bully friends among their number, sent sunshine falling into the room. It glistened on the black sewing machine that perched atop its refinished stand. The treadle was polished to a sheen, and the useless belts had been replaced with ones that were smooth and taut.

"Oh, my!" Doris put her hands up to her face. "You did it! You brought that old sewing machine back to life."

David, who looked so handsome in the plain clothes he now wore each day, said, "It works now. We fixed each piece of it and oiled it." He grinned. "Abby wound bobbins in every possible color of thread she could find. It's ready to go whenever you're ready to take it for a test-drive, Doris."

"Not me." The old woman linked her arm through her great-niece's. "I've had the sewing machine for a long time. Now it's time for a new owner. It's yours, Barbara."

Her niece's cheeks flushed with happiness

as the teens cheered. "They repaired it for you, Aunt Doris."

"No, I asked them to fix it up for you. Enjoy it. Use it." She winked as she added, "And if it breaks down, I know a good repairman."

Abby gave the women a chance to thank the teens, then herded them out. She didn't want to tire out Doris with the excitement.

The kids headed toward the school to watch the younger ones play baseball, leaving her and David alone as they were so seldom. He often traveled by hired van to take classes in what he'd need to know before he could begin baptism classes. She'd been overjoyed when Isaac offered to help. She hadn't been sure if her inflexible brother would be willing to accept David as her future husband, but Isaac had been his usual terse self.

"If he's going to learn to live a plain life, he needs to learn from someone who will teach him properly," Isaac had said without a hint of humor.

Her brother had been as *gut* as his word and taught David almost every day while Isaac helped lay new floors in the big barn for the apartments David hoped to make available to two low-income families. Any animosity between them had faded as they'd come to respect each other's skills and dedication to their tasks.

Walking side by side through the middle of

the village, Abby laughed along with David as he told her stories about his mistakes as he re-learned *Deitsch*.

"For some reason," he said, making her giggle more, "Isaac and Michael seem to believe I should learn the adult words for things instead of the toddler ones I remember."

They paused when they reached the empty lot where the old St. Pierre farmhouse had stood for almost two hundred years. The ruined covered bridge was a looming shadow over the road, but rumor suggested it soon would be repaired.

"Mikayla has decided what she wants to do with the land." David picked up a stone and tossed it into the shallow water. He spoke *Deitsch* slower than he did *Englisch*, but was getting better with practice. "She wants to donate it to the town for a picnic park. A park named Boyd St. Pierre Memorial Park."

"What a lovely tribute to her *daed*!" Abby laced her fingers among his as she leaned her head on his shoulder. "She has a home with you, so she doesn't need another."

"She told me that in the same breath when she announced she intended to dye her hair purple."

Abby laughed. "At least it's a color we plain women wear, so she and I will match." She grew serious. "David, have you heard from your parents yet?"

His parents were slowly recovering at their home in California, and their prognosis was excellent. Though they'd reported gaps in their short-term memories, they were getting better with assistance from *doktors* and therapists.

"Ja." He took an envelope out of his pocket and handed it to her.

"You want me to read it?"

"I think you should."

She lifted out the single sheet and unfolded it. The letter was brief, but she hadn't gotten past the second sentence before the page blurred in front of her teary eyes.

Taking it back, he read aloud, "'While our first choice for you wouldn't be the life you're choosing, son, we want you to be happy. A plain life wasn't for us, but we will pray that it brings you the happiness a good son like you deserves.'"

She wanted to dance with sparkling steps as the light did on the water. "Thank God He has opened your parents' hearts. What a *wunderbaar* blessing He has given you!"

"Given us, *liebling*." He enfolded her to him for a sweet kiss, and she knew that she'd been wise to follow both her heart's desire and her head's joy to love.

* * * * *

Dear Reader,

When something momentous happens, our lives can feel as if they're tumbling out of control. For David Riehl, his search for the truth brought him answers he never expected. He has to depend on faith to get his feet under himself again. He has good examples in front of him as his neighbors face uncertainty in the wake of the flood.

The Mennonite Disaster Service is a real organization that was established seventy years ago when a group of young people wanted to help others. MDS volunteers, who are both plain and *Englisch*, come primarily from the US and Canada and have helped rebuild homes and lives after disasters, usually weather-related or due to wildfires.

Visit me at www.joannbrownbooks.com. Look for my next book, again set in Evergreen Corners, Vermont, coming this summer.

Wishing you many blessings,
Jo Ann Brown

Get 4 FREE REWARDS!

We'll send you 2 FREE Books plus 2 FREE Mystery Gifts.

Harlequin Heartwarming Larger-Print books will connect you to uplifting stories where the bonds of friendship, family and community unite.

FREE Value Over **$20**

A SUMMER AMISH COURTSHIP
by Emma Miller
With her son's misbehavior interrupting classes, Amish widow Abigail Stoltz must join forces with the schoolmaster, Ethan Miller. But as Ethan tutors little Jamie, Abigail can't help but feel drawn to him...even as her son tries to push them apart. Can they find a way to become a forever family?

AMISH RECKONING
by Jocelyn McClay
A new client is just what Gail Lapp's horse transportation business needs to survive. But as the single mom works with Amish horse trader Samuel Schrock, she's pulled back into the world she left behind. And returning to her Amish life isn't possible if she wants to keep her secrets...

THE PRODIGAL COWBOY
Mercy Ranch • by Brenda Minton
After their daughter's adoptive mom passes away and names Colt West and Holly Carter as guardians, Colt's determined to show Holly he isn't the unreliable bachelor she once knew. But as they care for their little girl together, can the cowboy prove he'd make the perfect father...and husband?

HER HIDDEN HOPE
Colorado Grooms • by Jill Lynn
Intent on reopening a local bed-and-breakfast, Addie Ricci sank all her savings into the project—and now the single mother's in over her head. But her high school sweetheart's back in town and happy to lend a hand. Will Addie's long-kept secret stand in the way of their second chance?

WINNING BACK HER HEART
Wander Canyon • by Allie Pleiter
When his ex-girlfriend returns to town and hires him to overhaul her family's general store, contractor Bo Carter's determined to keep an emotional distance. But to convince her old boss she's home for good, Toni Redding needs another favor—a pretend romance. Can they keep their fake love from turning real?

AN ALASKAN TWIN SURPRISE
Home to Owl Creek • by Belle Calhoune
The last person Gabriel Lawson expects to find in town is Rachel Marshall—especially with twin toddlers in tow. Gabriel refuses to risk his heart again on the woman who once left him at the altar years ago. But can they overcome their past to consider a future? _____

ReaderService.com has a new look!

We have refreshed our website and we want to share our new look with you. Head over to ReaderService.com and check it out!

On ReaderService.com, you can:

- Try 2 free books from any series
- Access risk-free special offers
- View your account history & manage payments
- Browse the latest Bonus Bucks catalog

Don't miss out!

If you want to stay up-to-date on the latest at the Reader Service and enjoy more Harlequin content, make sure you've signed up for our monthly News & Notes email newsletter. Sign up online at ReaderService.com.

RS19